W9-BBZ-190

Other *Leisure* books by Douglas Clegg:

THE ABANDONED
NIGHTMARE HOUSE
FOUR DARK NIGHTS (Anthology)
THE HOUR BEFORE DARK
THE INFINITE
NAOMI
MISCHIEF
YOU COME WHEN I CALL YOU
THE NIGHTMARE CHRONICLES
THE HALLOWEEN MAN

Writing as Andrew Harper:

NIGHT CAGE
RED ANGEL

THE
ATTRACTION

DOUGLAS CLEGG

LEISURE BOOKS   NEW YORK CITY

A LEISURE BOOK®

April 2006

Published by

Dorchester Publishing Co., Inc.
200 Madison Avenue
New York, NY 10016

The Attraction copyright © 2004 by Douglas Clegg
The Necromancer copyright © 2003 by Douglas Clegg

ISBN 0-8439-5411-6

Printed in the United States of America.

Visit us on the web at www.dorchesterpub.com.

For Edward Lee, and Lee Seymour.
With thanks to Raul Silva, Don D'Auria,
and to the readers of my novels, novellas, and stories.
The author invites readers to get free screensavers,
e-books and video trailers at www.DouglasClegg.com.

THE
ATTRACTION

Chapter One

1

Out on an empty highway, it called.

The Brakedown Palace was a junk gas station in the middle of a desert nowhere and looked—from the outside—as if coyotes guarded it. Tumbleweeds had grown like barbed wire where it edged the old highway, and rattlesnakes had dug tunnels beneath its garage bays. Had it ever thrived? Had the highway ever been so well traveled that the warped curio emporium had once been a popular stop? The jackalope statue—that perversity of taxidermy—an idea of rabbit hell that involved mounting a dead jackrabbit and thrusting the twin spears of antelope horns into its head as if this were some new yet alien creature. Had this attracted tourists? The scorpions in the individual killing jars, suspended in a thick clear liquid that made them glow green under

1

fluorescent lights—was this a draw for the weary traveler at one time? The place even had a small statue of the Virgin Mary, stolen from some old churchyard, covered with the garlands of dried flowers in honor of those who had died in car crashes on the highway—those drunks and sleepers-at-the-wheel whose last moments were spent looking at this endless big empty, this wilderness of nothing, in the middle of the ass-crack of the universe. The cars—smashed or sometimes only slightly damaged, with broken windshields that still reflected death's face—sat near the garages. I remember a red-and-white convertible T-bird, a classic, but inside the vehicle, rust and rot and that whiff of perfume and whiskey still staining its torn seats.

This was the place, the dumping ground of all things ruined and useless, that held the greatest attraction I would ever come to know.

The great unspeakable mystery! The dark wonder of the ancient world!

You wouldn't think it would have any attraction, that place. You might have thought it was a "bad place" from the look of it.

Imagine it: an old dump of a gas station at the edge of hell's highway in the desert, the one with the half-torn billboards nearby that read, SEE THE UNSPEAKABLE WONDER OF THE ANCIENT WORLD! WHAT IS THE ATTRACTION? WHAT MYSTERY DOES IT HOLD?

2

Watch the desert. It is out there. This abomination. Watch along the ridge, over at that mesa, after sundown.

You can hear it sometimes when it's completely dark. So dark, even the stars have died out.

In the Southwest. In Arizona. Not among the cities and towns. Out where the scrub brush and ocotillo cactus take over the landscape. In those places where the tumbleweed blows through like a whisper of the past. The coyotes at twilight on the ridge of a mesa, their *ki-yi*s sing of something sinister, something unnatural. The nest of rattlers in the shade of the overhanging rock has been driven out into the bare flat sunlight. And something there at sunset, scuttling along the dark lip of a cave—a crack in the wall of a cliff—some creature there.

Strange things live on the desert.

Strange people, too.

I heard from an old man over in town that some dogs had gotten torn up bad out on the mesa, right near where the new housing development was going in. Maybe it was just coyotes, or maybe even a mountain lion from up in the hills, driven down from its home by hunger and thirst. But it didn't sound like it.

Someone said that they found a deep hole in the ground when they started to dig up an area for a new house and a swimming pool. They break up the earth, tear into it, and change it. They don't think there's anything in that desert earth, do they? They don't think the something waits.

They're idiots to expand this town out there, out where nobody in his or her right mind should live.

3

What are the demons that drive us?

For me, it's the past. Memory is my demon. When we are young, we do stupid things. There's no way around it. Perhaps we experiment with a drug that will hurt us. Perhaps we attach ourselves to the wrong people for us. Perhaps we take the one road off to the side of the main highway that may be the one road we should never have taken. Some of us die from our stupid things. Some of us survive and look back and regret our youths.

Some of us have a feeling of being damned from our stupid choices when young.

But I found out that every man can be redeemed. No matter how awful his demons are. No matter what he has done. Murder? Redeemed! Betrayal? Redeemed. Witness to slaughter? Redeemed.

But sometimes redemption looks a lot like hell itself.

And those demons are still there. We chase them down, whether we wish to do so or not.

What makes us pursue those demons, even when they destroy us?

It's simply attraction. Once we get something in our eye, we want to see more of it. We want to own it.

Let me tell you about attraction.

Attraction makes us chase what, in the end, may chase us down. It is the shiny thing in the road that draws us, like crows, to our doom. Most times, the truck out of nowhere bears down on us and we end our lives in a flutter of dark feathers and scraped skin. Now and then, we nab the shiny thing and we fly with it. But there's always one more shiny thing on some other road. Attraction is like that.

I know about attraction. It led me to bad places, but also to good.

Once, after a two-year love affair with the bottle, a failed suicide attempt, and a growing realization that my life was my own and didn't belong to anyone else, I saw a woman walking down Main Street in Naga, Arizona, who looked like she kept two bobcats fighting under her dress. I followed her around town until she made it to her car, and then she turned around. I knew she was my redeemer the moment I saw her. It was more than attraction. It was something I didn't think, then, could exist in the universe.

It was grace.

She had a face that made me forget everyone else I had ever met. I found her attractive, to say the least. I would have chased her to the ends of the earth if I had to, and given that Naga, Arizona, seemed like the end of the earth, I suppose I did. I was just twenty-three at the time, and living a crazy life. But she decided I was right for her. We ended up getting married, I became a better man, and after she died—too young—I went and built my home in a cavern out along a mesa, about ten miles off the new highway. I hated people, didn't love the world, and preferred the company of jackrabbit and coyote to humankind. I had enough, and what I didn't have, I scavenged and hunted and traded for. I wrote books, some of which have been published, but few have been read. Books with titles like, *Abominations in the Ancient World*, and *The Lost Gospel of Hell*. I know things that most men don't, and I've tried to research all of it, to find out the truth of it. Sometimes, the visions themselves tell me the truth.

Sometimes, they lie.

I've seen a lot of strange things on the desert. I've seen a man who seemed to be turning into a dog. I've seen rains come out of nowhere, and from their pools, in the crater depressions of the mesa, strange fish generate from fossilized eggs. I've heard of a snake so large that it feeds on wild burros, and of a mountain lion that hunts only children.

But the one thing that is undoubtedly the

strangest in my existence was something called Scratch, something that lay within a stone box in a glass case inside a gas station's roadside attraction.

Let me tell you.

PART ONE

LET'S GO BACK TO THE 70s,
SHALL WE?

Chapter Two

1

1977. No cell phones. An old-fashioned, pre-tech world, if you will. An innocent world that seemed guilty. A year of death, pardon, disco, and, as the year wore on, gas lines. The death penalty was reinstated with the execution of Gary Gilmore, the first man to be executed in the U.S. of A. since 1967. Gerald Ford, then-president, pardoned Tokyo Rose. Pardons were the order of the day. Jimmy Carter, from the peanut-farming family, arrived in the White House just about the time when the economy began taking a downturn. Soon enough, gas lines lengthened. It was a strange year of unrest and discontent, and nobody knew why.

If you were in college at the time, and it was a little private middle-of-nowhere college in Virginia, in the mountains, you probably were a preppie, and you probably were in a fraternity, and you wanted to get the hell out of there except your folks were divorced, nobody really wanted you home for spring break, half your friends were heading to Virginia Beach, half to Florida, but the girl you wanted badly was going to make a fast trip to California and get back to campus within two weeks.

You owned a car and wanted to drive her out there and back. Four days out, four days back, four days in L.A.

Not bad.

It was a crazy thing to do.

But you were nineteen, hated your life, and crazy was something you needed.

She was someone you needed.

"Attraction can really fuck you up," Josh said.

He'd stretched out on the lawn because he drank too much that night and felt too awful and wished he were somewhere else and could be someone other than Josh, first to go to college on a scholarship, no less, and further from his dreams than he was from the stars above him.

2

Night descended, then grew luminous with the lights of the college and town. Jackson College, liberal arts, private, over-priced, party school.

It was one of those genteel colleges, nestled in the Blue Ridge, with columns and Old South delusions and tradition fermenting in the over-crowded boxwoods and magnolia overhangs. The town was quaint and small enough to support a single movie theater called the Bijou, and after nine o'clock, all the traffic lights flashed yellow. Fraternity Row was on a street called Willow Avenue. The houses looked as if they were all built the same year, with colonial columns and balconies, and a grandness all mushed nearly side-by-side: Lambda Chi, Deltas, Pi Phi, Zeta Beta. The frat houses all lined up in perfect rows, and on this particular Friday night, all were lit up with parties and drunken students and dance music blasting out of the open windows.

Josh, nineteen, lay back on the lawn in front of the Delta house, looking up at the stars.

He tried to identify the constellations—the Pleiades, Orion, Scorpio—but he nearly flunked astronomy. To him, they just looked like pin-pricks in the fabric of the world. The darkness, with the holes in it that hinted at another side—a bright paradise somewhere far away.

He was drunk on the cheapest beer from a warm keg out back in the driveway, and he'd stumbled to the front lawn, where girls stepped over him on the way into the party.

The party roared—its music and screams spreading out into the night, but he heard it like the ocean in a seashell at his ear.

It was both distant and close, and all he thought about was the girl he wished would be his.

"Attraction can really fuck you up," he said to no one. "It can mess you up good. You gotta choose the right person, because if you don't, and you choose the wrong one, or you let nature take over so you always pick the wrong ones, it sends you to hell. Hell in a handbasket."

He thought of Bronwyn.

3

Bronwyn Shapiro: brown hair that was straight and long, five-foot-three, wore black too much, smoked too much, no breasts to speak of, but somehow was more skeletally advanced than other sophomores. She wore glasses but looked intellectual instead of geeky, didn't put up with any crap from the guys at the frat, wrote poetry that she considered puerile but she took creative writing classes, anyway. That's where Josh first saw her: freshman year, Expository and Creative Writing 101, Michael Framington—the short story writer—teaching. Bronwyn read a poem about setting fire to her roommate's hair. Framington called it the worst case of overwrought emotional baggage with the sensibility of a disturbed eighteen-year-old that he'd heard in years.

Josh wanted to hear it again.

After that class, he went to her and asked her what she was reading. She glanced up at him from the tamped-down carpet of fresh grass. Then she shut the book, tucking it under her arm.

"It's called a book," she said.

"Now that's a suitably bitchy thing to say," he said.

"You know, when I've noticed you in class, I've always thought you were a loser and now you've just confirmed it for me," she said. "Please leave."

And that was the moment he felt that he had to have this woman in his life no matter what.

A year later, lying on the grass, looking up at the stars, Josh wished she were with him.

4

Bronwyn sat on the stairs, nursing a beer, and wishing she were anywhere else but in a frat house the night after second-semester finals.

"See him?" she nudged her friend, Alli. Her target was Mitchell Sloane, from Poughkeepsie, New York, wearing his cardigan and khakis, vodka gimlet in one hand, cigar in another. "He's a classic closet case. His friends think he's male bonding or something, but look at how he's sizing up Joe Welsh. He wants to plant a big wet one on Joe's puss."

"Half these frat boys are closet cases," her friend said.

"How'd you do on the accounting final?"

"Okay, I think."

"I bit the dust," Bronwyn said. "I thought that last question about debits and credits was a trick question. I wrote a note to Jones that he was trying to trick us on the final and that the answer was that it was impossible. I think I just flunked. Look at him." She pointed with the bottle toward Dave Olshaker. "He's pathetic. He's looking for Tammy Detweiler."

"The hose queen," Alli said.

"Exactly. He thinks she must love him just because he gets a boner when he looks at her."

"Detweiler's incapable of love."

"So's Olshaker. Maybe they're made for each other. Besides, Olshaker's a psycho, and him," Bronwyn's bottle tipped over to a guy with filthy long hair and dirty jeans and a stained T-shirt.

"He looks like a scrappy dog."

"Ziggy. He's just looking for weed. He dropped acid seventeen times before he was eighteen. You can be declared legally insane for that. He's legally insane too many times over. But hell, he's got a light. I need a light."

5

"Where's Griff?" Bronwyn asked, leaning over Kathy Emmons to light her cigarette from Ziggy's magical torch.

Ziggy gave a blank look. "No idea."

"God, this cigarette tastes like pure unadulterated . . . poop." Bronwyn took another drag off the cigarette, then stubbed it out against the wall of the frat house. "He's with her, isn't he?"

Kathy nodded. "Of course."

"Damn it," Bronwyn said. She let out a vile string of profanity, but her curses couldn't be heard above the thud of the music on the floor below.

"Let's get high," Ziggy said.

"You're already high. Give up the drugs, Ziggy. I'm telling you. You are going to mess up your entire life and maybe even your chromosomes so your future wife might have turtle babies someday. You're going to end up in rehab anyway. Just stop now. 'High' is not the natural state for human beings. Low is. Get low. Low is good."

"I want to get high," Ziggy said, as if he hadn't heard a word. He glanced at the others, then wandered off, claiming that he'd left a bong somewhere in the kitchen.

"Why are you obsessed with Griff?" Kathy asked. "He dumped you."

"No," Bronwyn said. "I dumped him."

"Okay. Either way, a dumping was had by all. Many moons ago."

"I don't give a damn about him," Bronwyn said. "I just don't get what he sees in Tammy. Jesus, she has him, and Olshaker wants her back. What is it about her? She's the poster girl for the living dead. Is it just boobies? Is that all boys are about? Boobies?"

"I think so."

"Yeah, sadly, sometimes I think so, too," Bronwyn said, her cigarette nearly gone to ash. "Sometimes I wish I didn't give a damn."

6

A room upstairs in the frat house. Smell of beer and sex in the room. Tammy on top of Griff Montgomery. His pants around his ankles, which dangle over the edge of the slender bed. His starched white button-down shirt open at the chest.

Tammy's jeans on the floor, her tank top half-pulled up around her neck, the small gold cross that hung from her neck bouncing up and down as her thighs wrap around, obscuring and engulfing Griff.

"God, do you feel my big boy?" he asked, too loud.

"Uh?"

"My big boy," he repeated. "Do you feel it? I feel like . . . like I'm God or something. It feels so big."

"Uh," Tammy muttered, "uh, sure. Yeah. Sure. Anything you say."

"Don't you like it? Tell me how much you like it."

"Oh yeah, I like it. I love it."

"Say it."

"No. You know I don't want to."

"Aw, please. Baby. It does so much for me."

"Okay. Okay. Your . . . big boy. Your big boy is so good." She began giggling a little, but he didn't notice.

"Oh yeah. Oh yeah!" he groaned against her ear as she leaned into him.

"It's the biggest one I ever had. It's the biggest. I don't know if I can take it all. Oh," she whispered. "Oh."

In her head, Tammy was thinking about how she worked too hard and how he needed to move around some more.

7

In his head, Griff was thinking about two other girls at school, and pretending that it was both of them, kissing him, taking him into themselves, flicking their tongues all over him, and whispering obscenities like they were good luck charms.

8

They thrashed, and finally, they fell over on the floor, a heap in the heap of dirty laundry that Griff left there.

She didn't kiss him afterward, but got up, pulled on her panties, and looked in the long mirror on the door to his room. "I think I'm getting fat."

Griff, lying on the dirty clothes, some of which bunched up uncomfortably under his lower back, considered whether he should shower.

Without saying another word, he bounded out of bed, grabbing a towel from the heap of dirty clothes in the corner by the dresser. He picked up his shirt, jeans, and briefs, gave her a wink and a too-brief hug, and went out into the hall.

9

In the shower, one floor down from his room, Griff took the Ivory soap and scrubbed away. Tammy had this smell that he couldn't stand. When it got on him, it reminded him too much of his mother's closet where he used to hide, and he hated that smell.

Then he thought of someone else, someone other than Tammy, and he got hard again.

10

"You whore," Dave Olshaker said.

He stood in the doorway of Griff's room, staring at Tammy.

Chapter Three

1

Dave Olshaker had been waiting on the stairs, and when he saw Griff run out to the showers, he knew he had his chance. He slammed the door shut behind him. Reached back, and twisted the bolt.

He was a big guy, maybe 240, six five, like L'il Abner in overalls and a white T-shirt, a townie who had a scholarship to Jackson College. He looked, to Tammy Detweiler, as pissed as anyone could be. He turned his back to her for a second, fiddling with the lock on the door.

"Dave? What the hell are you doing in here?"

"You slept with that idiot," Olshaker said, turning around to face her. "You told me you loved me."

"That was last year. Dave? Get the hell out of here. I'll scream."

"You won't. You can't do this to me. You

21

whore. You know I gave you my heart. And now you're just stomping all over it. Look, look, I forgive you. Okay? I forgive you for your transgression, baby. I do. I love you that much."

"You aren't gonna forgive me for anything. Now get the hell out of here, right now."

Tammy leapt out of bed, forgetting that she was bare-ass naked. She felt like trying to find the gun Griff kept. She was pretty sure it was in the top drawer of his dresser. He wasn't supposed to have it, but then in college you weren't supposed to have a lot of things you ended up having.

Olshaker rushed her, grabbing her by the wrists. "Just come back to me. Just tell me."

She was shocked to see tears in his eyes. "Let go of me, damn it!"

His face turned bright red. He was angry. She knew the look—it was half the reason they'd broken up before midterms. He had slapped her a little too hard, and she had seen that red face. He was scary sometimes.

Her wrists hurt where he gripped her. "Let me go. Please," she said more calmly, looking down at his hands. "Please. You're hurting me, David."

"I just want you," he said. His breath was all sour beer. Right then and there, he began blubbering like a baby. He released her wrists. She shoved him backward, and he fell, ass-first, on Griff's bed. "You don't know what it's like. To love someone so much. To love them, to want them, you just don't know. Honey, honey, I love you. I love you like no man is ever gonna love you." His tears came in hiccups and heaves. She began to feel bad for him, despite everything. Once she was dressed, she went over to the bed, and sat beside him. She put her arm around his back.

"Look. You're a good man," she said, but felt as if she were telling the biggest lie on the planet. "You'll find a girl who loves you because you're wonderful. I'm no good. I really am not right for you. Maybe I'm not right for anyone. But you, you have a lot going for you."

"I know," he said, weeping bitterly. "I know. But I can save you from your sinful life, Tammy. I can make you a good woman."

"Poor baby," Tammy said, hugging him to her. "Poor, poor baby."

"I love you," he said.

He looked up at her with his tear-stained face. He looked like a puppy dog that had just been hit by a car and lived to whimper about it. He leaned in to kiss her, and she felt badly enough for him that she let him.

And that's when he grabbed her and drew her in to him, and thrust his tongue between her lips. She pushed him away, but his grip snaked around her arms and waist like a straitjacket. He maneuvered to the side, and brought her down on the bed, turning her around so that her face pressed into the blanket. "You know I love you," he said, slobbering. "You know you're my woman."

She tried to cry out, but her mouth was gagged with the blanket.

She felt him grind against her.

2

In what was called the Persian Room, in the basement of the frat house—a small room full of a haze of blue smoke—Ziggy sucked on a bong while clouds of sweet smoke billowed around him. Somebody said, "You look like a fire-breathing dragon, Zigster."

Ziggy laughed and felt his face go all red. He wondered whether he'd ever been this high before. He looked at his hands to make sure they weren't sprouting leaves. For a second, he thought he was turning into a tree.

"What's up with that?" he asked his partner-in-high, Joe Metheny.

"With what?"

"My hands? It's like they're ripping out of my arms."

"Holy shit."

Both of them laughed at once. Then stopped. Then laughed again.

There were others in the haze of smoke, but Ziggy only noticed Joe, who had the most hilarious look on his face—a red smile and a sparkling around his eyes.

"You know what I like about you?"

"What's that?"

"You're always happy," Ziggy said. Then he took another hit from the Monster Bong.

3

"Where the hell is Josh?" Bronywn picked her way through the rabble of the party—students passed out on the floor, others leaning into their girl-friend's face in the corners of rooms, still others managed to keep dancing to music that had stopped ten minutes before. All the while the stench of beer and vomit, up and down the stairs—and just as she got to the top of the stairs, coming out of the bathroom, naked, in full swing, Griff.

She felt as if she'd been shot with a ray gun and couldn't move.

She tried not to look at him. He was a golden Apollo. His hair was slicked back on his scalp, and it emphasized his high cheekbones and his pool-blue eyes and the way his nose was the slightest of ski-slopes. She couldn't help herself—she looked down at his chest, developed from football and wrestling, and then along his abs, the striation of muscle prominent, his pale skin slick with water.

The millisecond passed. He didn't notice her watching, and passed by the stairs, heading back to his room.

Bronwyn caught her breath and sat down on the stairs. Another cigarette, this time for several long, drawn-out puffs.

The doorway at the top of the stairs went to one

of the upperclassman's rooms. It was open, and she got up and walked through it to the balcony. She went out to the edge of the balcony and looked up at the stars that were just fading as morning came up along the horizon in a new day that was still too distant from the night.

When she glanced down at the murky front lawn, she saw a guy she was pretty sure was Josh.

4

"You're drunk," she said. She crouched down in the dew-wet grass beside his prone body. "I hate drunks."

"No, I'm not," he said. "I'm star-gazing."

"You didn't touch any booze?" She kicked at the empty bottle of Jack Daniels at his side.

"Okay. Busted. Just a little."

"Damn it. We go in three hours. Why do you boys get so drunk? What was so awful in your cushy little lives that you have to screw it up by becoming instant alcoholics once you leave Mommy and Daddy behind?"

He opened his mouth, about to answer, but she said, "No, I don't want to know. Really. Drunk or stoned, it's like all of you are getting anaesthetized to the pain of being upper-middle class."

"I'm on scholarship."

"That doesn't make you poor. You own a car. None of you lives in the real world. Good God," she said, shaking her head. "Good God." She glanced at her watch. "We're never getting on the road at this rate."

"I'm ready."

"We're never getting to L.A."

"We'll get there. I drove from Chicago to Atlanta in one night once. We can get to L.A. in three days. At the most, four. I promise. How many people are coming?"

"Total, five. I think. You, me, Griff, Tammy, and maybe Ziggy if he doesn't get too messed up tonight. Everybody chips in, so it's a free trip for you. You're the scholarship boy. Packed in like sardines in that junk-heap you call a car."

"That'll be cozy," he said, laughing.

"You need to sleep this off before we go. Damn it," she said. "God, drinking is stupid."

"Hey, you smoke."

She nodded, and as if this had reminded her, reached over and opened the small leather pouch that served as her purse, and drew out a fresh pack of cigarettes. When she finally tapped one out, lighting it, she said, "Smoking is different."

"It's a nasty habit."

"Maybe," she said, seriously considering this as she took a long drag off the cigarette. "You may be on to something there."

"You want to see Orion?" he asked. He pointed to a group of white specks in the dark sky. "Come on. Lie down. Here, use my jacket. There. Now, look."

"That's not Orion."

"Okay, it's something else. It's the unnamed star. Let's connect the dots and make them into somebody."

"Like who?"

"There's Ziggy," Josh said, drawing an invisible line with his finger, swooping it in the air from a cluster of stars to a single bright one. "See, he's got his bong."

"I see it," she said. "And there's Tammy. See the boobs?"

5

Josh made a wish on the last star, just before it extinguished.

Bronywn drifted to sleep beside him, her last cigarette falling on the wet grass as morning arrived.

They both woke up at the same time, hours later, in the afternoon on Saturday with Josh's arm slipped beneath Bronwyn's neck. He opened his eyes and knew, instinctively, that she had also just woken. She sat up, drawing away from him. Glanced at her watch. "We're already late. Please tell me the Pimpmobile is running okay."

6

Ziggy had an acid-flashback tripticular dream, and in it something small and nasty with eyes like green stones on fire and claws like shiny black hooks leapt for him like it was a jaguar from hell.

He awoke and drank an entire pot of coffee before going off in search of the others about to leave on the road trip that would get him away from the drugs for awhile.

He hoped.

But all he could think about, wired on coffee, were the nasty eyes of that little bastard he saw in his dreams.

7

The Pimpmobile was more than its name could ever suggest. Not just a car but a boat on wheels. A big fat honkin' Lincoln Town Car sedan. Given to Josh by his grandmother when he went to college. She drove her cars hard and put them up cracked and dried out, and often was in accidents, so something always went wrong—a headlight that blinked, a strange push on the brakes, something about the shotgun seat that didn't feel entirely comfortable. Small problems that could be worked around. His grandmother was named Alfreda, and she used to fart in the car so much that Josh was sure it still had her stink. She had died soon after giving him the car—her smoking and drinking got the better of her—and he missed her. He kept the car, even though it was held together by duct tape and got about ten miles to the gallon. Even though it had some issues—it was a little low in the trunk, and the backseat was covered with tape and smelled permanently like cigarette ash, and there was this noise the car made every few miles that sounded like the squeal of a cat getting hit. Josh took care of the Pimpmobile. He had spent all of Thursday, not studying for his Early American History final, but washing and waxing and tuning up the boat for the big trip.

Here's how the trip evolved: back in February, Bronwyn's dad and his new wife moved to L.A. from Chicago. Bronwyn hated the new wife but loved her dad, and even though her dad didn't want to see her, she told him she was coming for spring break come hell or high water.

Josh's Pimpmobile was the only ride she could get.

"I can pay all gas," she told him. "And two nights in a motel."

"You don't have to do that," Josh said.

She looked at him strangely. "Yeah—I do. It'll take four nights at the most. But I know we can make it in under three if we take turns driving. Plus, I've got a radar detector. We can go 100 on some of the desert roads. They're straight lines with no traffic at four in the morning, and I love drinking a pot of coffee and driving through them before the sun comes up. Plus, we can get other people to pitch in on gas."

Because Griff and Tammy and Ziggy were going to go too the car would be packed, but Bronwyn claimed the shotgun seat three weeks before the trip. The day of the trip—which turned into Saturday evening—the only person who hadn't shown up at the designated spot was Ziggy, and they had to drive around for forty minutes before they found him in the college library, asleep on one of the leather couches.

He opened his eyes to see all four of them standing over him.

"What the hell?" he asked.

"I don't love druggies," Bronwyn said as she took a long, last drag off a dying cigarette. "I just don't like it." She pointed down at him. "No weed goes on this trip. Understood? Beer's fine, although no drinking and driving. No drugs."

"Beer's a drug," Ziggy moaned, scratching himself under the arms like a dog after fleas.

Bronwyn squinted and pursed her lips. "I think you know what I mean."

The road trip began about an hour later, and for a while nobody said a word—as if none of them was sure they'd get along for the entire drive to the West Coast.

By nine they were on the main highway toward Tennessee.

Chapter Four

1

It took too long to get through the South, let alone reach the Southwest.

Josh drove first shift, then Bronwyn, then Griff. After Griff's six hours' were up, he got in the backseat and, without anyone being aware of it, put Tammy's hands on the bulge in his pants and whispered in her ear that she should just keep stroking it. Tammy pretended she was getting the little bottle of Vaseline moisturizer from her handbag because her hands were drying out. Ziggy pretended to be asleep, but he told Josh later how, when Josh was driving and Bronwyn was talking a mile a minute about why Ayn Rand was the most brilliant human being who had ever lived, Tammy had unzipped Griff and given him a slow, easy hand job that had driven Ziggy nearly crazy as he watched through his nearly closed eyes. "He's a big boy," Ziggy told Josh later, when they got out to pump gas. "And Tammy was licking his ear the whole time she did it. Man, he is one lucky dude."

"Too much information," Josh said.

"He's like the Alpha."

"What?"

"The Alpha. Like in wolf packs. One male gets the hot chicks. All the other males—that's you and me—never get laid."

"I get laid."

"Yeah, sure."

"No, I do."

"That's why you're all alone on this trip. Like me," Ziggy said. Then, Ziggy sniffed his fingers. "God, even my fingers smell like sex. I can't believe you and Bron didn't notice. It was freaky."

"Sleazy's more like it."

"Ah, you're just jealous," Zig said, and then went to use the restroom at the back of the gas station.

Josh glanced at Tammy, who was just going into the ladies' room. Griff stood outside it, grinning, his hands in his pocket. Then, thinking nobody was watching, he tapped on the door to the ladies' room.

The door opened.

Griff went inside.

Bronwyn was still in the car, smoking. Josh went over to her side. "Guess who had sex in the backseat today?"

"Please tell me this didn't involve you and Ziggy in some way."

He shot her a look. "Griff and Tammy."

Bronwyn's eyes seemed to squint into tiny cuts, then opened wider. "That whore. She just traps men with sex. That's all it is."

"Yeah," Josh said.

"Like you're any different."

"I am."

Bronwyn smiled, blew out a puff of smoke, and touched the edge of his wrist. "No, you are. You're so different I thought you might be gay when I first met you."

"Gay? I'm not gay."

"Don't get all defensive. It was the poetry you wrote. For creative writing. It was sensitive. That's all. Not like the way other guys write stuff that's all about them and their exploits. You wrote about something different."

Oh Christ, he thought. *Oh Christ. She sees me as a dickless wonder.*

"I think they're going at it in there," he said, nodding toward the restroom.

"Gross." Bronwyn sucked back some smoke, then heaved it out in a long sigh. She leaned forward into the dashboard, stubbing her cigarette out in the ashtray. "Let me tell you something, Josh. Something about some girls. There are these girls like Tammy that boys really like because of this whole sex issue. But girls know about who she really is. She's a sad pathetic idiot who thinks her whole life should revolve around giving the worst kind of men what they want."

"You're just saying that because of him. Griff. You still want him."

"Once. Maybe. Not anymore. I don't think I could ever want someone who slept with some of the girls he's slept with. Back when I dated him, you know, he'd only slept with a few girls. At this point, the numbers are reaching the populations of small island nations. Tammy's just one of many, I'm sure."

"You don't fool me," he said. "Not one bit. You like bad boys. Nice girl like you, rich family. It's true, isn't it?"

"Bite me, preppie boy," she said.

2

Nobody thought Tammy should drive because she had too many beers during the day, and Ziggy somehow managed to get stoned, even though no one could specifically say when he did it. It was assumed he went into the bathroom at HoJo's or Stuckeys or the Waffle Huts, and just got high fast.

They stopped six times the first day because Tammy had to pee so much. Or else, as Josh and Ziggy assumed, she and Griff had to sexually christen every sleazoid gas station bathroom in the Bible Belt. They drove through Memphis with Griff telling a story about how he got lost in downtown Memphis once and went to some big party there and passed out and woke up the next day in New Orleans. He thought it was a funny story, but no one laughed. Then, in Little Rock, Bronwyn called her father collect. He told her that she was an idiot to plan a trip like this with people she didn't know and that he'd send a plane ticket if she wanted to come out. She hung up on him, and chain-smoked the rest of the day and evening, which got them to Oklahoma City, where they all crashed in one room at a Howard Johnson's. They slept for eleven hours, until the maids finally banged on the door the next afternoon, trying to get them up and out.

They went from Oklahoma down through the Texas Panhandle, and Ziggy wanted to stop at El Paso for something, and that's where things started to go seriously wrong. Griff and Tammy wanted to spend a day in Juarez bar-hopping, and Bronwyn's period had started (she didn't need to announce it, everyone knew when she went into snapping turtle mode), and Josh had to go rescue Griff from a fight at a badly lit bar, even though Griff had been the creep who was coming on to other men's wives in the bar.

"What the hell are you doing?" Josh asked, yanking Griff by his wrinkled button-down shirt, out from the darkness of the bar, into the searing white light of midday. Griff crumbled to the ground, shielding his face as if expecting to get hit one more time.

"I'm havin' a little fun. You know about fun?"

Griff giggled, and wiped a smidgeon of blood from the edge of his lips.

"That guy could've done some serious damage to you."

Griff raised his eyebrows in a "who cares?" attitude, and reached his hand up to Josh. "Come on, help me up."

Josh gave him a lift up, and smacked him lightly on the back of the head. "Get back to the car. Jesus, now I've got to go back in there and get Tammy. Could you just stay out of trouble once in your life?"

"This isn't trouble," Griff replied, stumbling off in search of the others in the car, parked out on the main road. "The lacrosse trophies. Now that was trouble."

Who could forget? Josh thought. Who could forget someone having stolen all the lacrosse trophies at Jackson College that had been won over the past ten years, the prize sport of Jackson. Why the Gods of Jackson had played lacrosse. Griff and his frat brothers had stolen all of them, then pissed in them, and left them in front of Dean Egan's house at the edge of campus. Griff was a moron and a thief, and he'd been like this since as long as Josh had known him—which was only two years now.

3

In Las Cruces, New Mexico, they got pulled over by the cops. Griff told Bronwyn to show the cop her boobs so they wouldn't get the ticket. "My sister did that once. She had these big boobies. And I was riding shotgun, and this cop pulled her over for going 85 in a 55 zone. She just unbuttoned her blouse three inches down and acted all babylike, and he didn't give her a ticket. It works. Honest."

They saw the first billboard before they reached the eastern edge of Arizona. None of them really noticed it at first. Only Ziggy. He had been smoking a joint for lunch, and started laughing after they'd passed it.

"What'd it say?" Tammy asked.

"Something about the Unspeakable."

"Unspeakable? What the hell is 'unspeakable' supposed to mean? You can't speak it or something?"

"Exactly," Bronwyn said, only nobody detected the bitchiness in her tone.

"Something unspeakable and unknown. An ancient wonder of the world. Coming up somewhere. Off some exit," Ziggy added.

Ziggy kept complaining that he couldn't sleep because of all the bumps they hit in the road, so Bronwyn had them stop the car. She went to the trunk, opened it, and drew out a couple of blankets. She rolled one up for Ziggy's pillow and threw the other one over him for comfort, although it was a warm day. Ziggy closed his eyes soon after, and they all snickered a little as he snored. Then, suddenly, he let out a bloodcurdling scream, to the point where Griff nearly pulled the car off the road.

Ziggy glanced around: They all stared at him. "I had a nightmare," he said.

4

The second sign stood about fifty miles farther up the highway among a mass of billboards about trading posts and outlet malls in Tucson. This time, Josh read it aloud as it went by, "Come see the mystery! The great ancient wonder! The Unspeakable, Unknowable Attraction! The Secret of the Ancient Aztecs!"

Then, he read off the last bit, about mileage and turn-offs to get to the site, "Hey, we're apparently only two hundred miles from the great mystery of the asshole of the universe."

"I love those kinds of places," Bronwyn said. "When I used to travel with my dad, we'd stop at all of the roadside attractions. Sometimes they were just rattlesnakes in cages. Sometimes they had what looked like babies in jars."

"I saw John Dillinger's dong once," Griff said.

"Bull."

"I did. It was in this museum in D.C. It was so

big they kept it in this long jar. Just floating in this formaldehyde gunk."

"Nasty," Ziggy said. "That's nasty. You die and then they cut off your dick and stick it in a museum."

"Don't worry, Zig. Yours is safe," Griff laughed. "There's no itty-bitty museum."

"I want to go see the unspeakable and unknowable attraction," Bronwyn said, flicking her cigarette out the window. She stretched out, and pressed her bare feet up against the dashboard. Josh looked at her feet, and noticed that they were small and perfect, with toes that didn't intrude on each other, as his did.

"What route was it on?"

"No idea," Josh said, watching the road, watching her feet.

That night, in Tucson, they stayed at the cheapest motel they could find (The Roadrunner Inn). Josh sat up to watch the news and then Johnny Carson before drifting off to sleep with his face not far enough away from Ziggy's smelly feet.

Nerves were shot by the time they got back on the highway the next morning. Griff insisted on driving, and nobody had gotten a good night's sleep in the motel because Ziggy was sick and the toilet wouldn't flush and the smell alone kept them awake, to say nothing of the broken-down air-conditioning and the way the heat had shot up sometime after crossing Texas to New Mexico, and then, at its worst, into Arizona.

On the road, Ziggy kept having them stop because he got carsick every few miles.

5

Bronwyn spotted another billboard for the Unknowable Mystery, and this time it was more explicit.

YOU'RE NEAR THE MYSTERY! THE UNKNOWABLE, UNSPEAKABLE TERROR OF THE ANCIENT WORLD IS JUST DOWN ROUTE 19 AT THE BRAKEDOWN PALACE AND SUNDRIES. NAVAJO BLANKETS! TURQUOISE! ARROWHEADS! FIREWORKS!

"I intend to be the unspeakable, unknowable mystery of the modern world," Bronwyn said, and Josh watched as she closed her eyes gently. He thought she was the prettiest girl he had ever seen.

Josh knew he shouldn't shut his eyes and lean against Bronwyn and fall asleep. But he couldn't help it.

6

He dreamed that he and Bronwyn were in a deep green forest. The trees towered over them, like a cathedral of nature. The fern beneath their feet was like a bed. Bronwyn began to undress, stepping out of her panties, finally, and he began to feel her all over. She gyrated against his touch, and soon his clothes had fallen away, and Bronwyn went on her hands and knees. She glanced up at him, smiling. He took her there, on the fern, on a soft mossy floor. He felt the intense pleasure of warm wet heat when he went inside her, and she began whispering something about how he needed to wake up now. Only he didn't want to wake up.

Then something shifted in the woods, and the trees began to vanish, one by one. He didn't care, because he felt so good inside Bronwyn, but soon, they were in an open space, and it was not Bronwyn beneath him at all, but Griff who said, "This isn't trouble, Josh. Don't worry. This is good times!"

That's when he woke up.

7

"Holy shit," someone said.

Reality banged against him. Light of day. Heat in the car. Leaning against Ziggy now instead of Bronwyn.

The car had come to a stop in what seemed to be a ditch.

Chapter Five

1

"What the hell were you thinking?" Bronwyn shouted from the backseat. She lit up a cigarette.

Josh glanced from her to Griff, who sat behind the steering wheel. It was almost as if cartoon steam came out of his ears. Griff wouldn't turn around and face the backseat.

Tammy, however, would. "You bitch, just shut your hole. All of us were sleeping. We're all too damn tired. And somebody stinks. Who stinks?"

Josh glanced at Ziggy, who shrugged. "Don't look at me, dude."

Griff pressed his face down, almost to the steering wheel.

"What happened?"

"Mister I-Can-Drive-Now fell asleep at the wheel," Bronwyn said. She lit a cigarette and sucked back the first smoke and then spat a ghost trail of it out into the already smoky car.

Josh—still half asleep, his back soaked with sweat, feeling cranky and sore from the position he'd formed on the hump of the backseat between Bronwyn and Ziggy—realized something. "Jesus. We're sideways."

"No shit, Sherlock."

"Didn't anybody notice?"

"I was snoozing," Ziggy said.

"I think we all were," Tammy said in that little-girl voice of hers that didn't quite go with the big boobs.

"Exactly," Bronwyn said. "Griff included."

"Shut your hole!" Tammy shouted. She got on her knees and swiveled around in her seat. Her face looked less like blond hose queen and more like pit bull with wig as she began listing all the ways Bronwyn sucked. "You're like the bitch queen of the universe with your 'I'm so sophisti-cated and together and I know everything and I look down on everybody'. And second, you are after Griff. Just say it. Just because he didn't care for you anymore, just because he dumped you—"

"Correction," Bronwyn said. "I dumped him."

"Look, Miss Perfect Bitch, he dumped you, be-cause you were too clingy and annoying and too much into proving everybody around you wrong. Why is that? Why is everybody else always

wrong? And don't sit there with that smug Jewish look."

"Excuse me?"

"You know what I mean, that 'Jewish Princess
from Intellectual Hell' look."

"That 'smug, Jewish look,'" Bronwyn repeated
slowly. "As opposed to your dumbass shiksa feeb
whiney anti-Semitic pigface?"

"You're jealous. You're jealous because I have
him. Because he wants me. Just admit it. Just admit it and get over it."

"First, admit that you're a raging anti-Semite
whose tits are bigger than her I.Q."

"Suck my dick," Tammy said, and then pushed
at the car door, opened it, and gingerly got out of
the car along the edge of the ditch. More obscenities flowed from her lips as she stomped off a
ways down the road.

Bronwyn, to her credit, took it all, enveloping
her face in a cloud of smoke; a mask through
which she could make sour faces back at Tammy
without being noticed.

"I didn't know Tammy was anti-Semitic," Josh
said to no one.

"Also anti-*semantic*," Bronwyn said. "She probably doesn't even know what it means."

Josh grinned, shaking his head, surveying the
damage. "We gotta get the car back on the
road."

Bronwyn, ignoring him, looked out across the

sky. "I hate you all. I hate this place. I wish we could just turn around and go home."

2

"Where the hell are we?" Josh asked. He stood outside the Lincoln, and glanced from the torn and twisted map of the U.S. to the lunar landscape surrounding them.

"Don't get mad at me!" Griff said. "It's not my fault! I took one turn."

"You took a turn?"

"I got tired of the highway."

"You *what?*" Josh asked.

"I thought Route 66 was here somewhere. I thought that's what the sign said."

"Did you go south or north?"

Griff shrugged, a hapless look on his face. "Maybe north."

"How long do you think you were driving like that?"

Griff closed his eyes, as if doing so could make him remember. Then he opened one eye. "Not sure. Maybe an hour? Maybe . . . maybe a half-hour?"

"All we have to do is turn around," Bronwyn said calmly. "If we're north. We just go that way." She pointed to what she assumed was south, then, glancing at the sun, adjusted slightly.

Josh thrust his hand out. "Give me those."

"Give you what? My smokes?"

Josh grabbed the pack of Merits from her hand.

He shook it violently until a cigarette popped out. He thrust it between his lips, and wrested the Bic lighter free from her grip. He spun the wheel until the small flame came up. He lit the cigarette.

Bronwyn glared at him, and then her face seemed to calm. "They're good for this kind of occasion," she said. "Even if they kill you."

"Everybody dies from something." He took a long draw of smoke into his lungs, coughing most of it back up. "All right. We need to figure out how to get the car back on the road. There are five of us. There's no reason in hell why we can't all get down on the other side of that ditch and push. We can bounce it back up."

"I'd say it would be a smarter use of daylight to go back to the highway. It can't be that many miles back, over that ridge." Bronwyn pointed with her cigarette. "Three of us stay here, two walk it. I don't mind a walk. I can walk ten miles, easy. It's not that hot. We go back and we flag someone for help. There's gas stations and rest stops all over the place on the 10."

"I'm boiling," Tammy said.

"I'm not walking twelve miles," Josh said. "Damn it."

"Me, neither," Griff said.

"I can do it. Ziggy?"

Ziggy shook his head. "I got bunions." Then, he added, "I inherited them from my grampa. Third-generation bunions."

Bronwyn looked at the others. "I'm not going

alone." Her eyes narrowed to slits as she stared at Griff.

"If we all work together," Josh said. "We can get the car out of the ditch."

Bronwyn looked at him with squinty eyes, her head cocked slightly to the side.

Quietly, she said, "So you really think we can get it back on the road?"

He glanced at the others, then back at Bronwyn. "Yes."

"It looks like we'd need a tow truck. Or some other kind of way to lift it."

Josh glanced back at the Lincoln, then at Bronwyn. He felt his heart racing, and he wasn't sure why since he wasn't panicked or all that worried. He felt something he hadn't generally felt in life. Something that no one had ever demanded of him. He felt as if he knew how to handle this.

"We can see-saw it up," he said.

"You study engineering?"

"I didn't have to," he said, grinning. "When I was four, I spent a lot of time on see-saws. I got the gist. Look, it'll take hours to walk back to the highway. If we all just pitch in, we can get out of this ditch and be on the road in less than an hour. I'm sure of it. And if it doesn't work, I'll walk with you. No, I'll do better than that. You can wait here and I will walk to the highway and get help."

Her face brightened, and she nodded, slowly. "Okay. But will you do me one favor?"

"What's that?"

"Don't pretend." She reached over and plucked the lit cigarette from his mouth and dropped it to the gravel. "You can't fake being a smoker. You can't fake anything."

3

Josh had been wrong.

It took the better part of two hours to get the car out of the ditch. Tammy whined, Ziggy was no real help at all, but Griff and Bronwyn both put some muscle into pushing, and when they finally got back on the road—with the sun going down a bit to the far western hills—the car made some funny rattling noises that Josh guessed originated somewhere in the rear axle.

Josh turned the Lincoln around and headed back toward what they hoped was the highway.

Instead, he found a confluence of ribbon roads, a narrow crossroads with what looked like pyramid-shaped hills in the distance and that strange cast of sulfurous light and purple shadow in the sagebrush, which meant night would seep across the desert roads within a few hours.

Without asking the others for their suggestions on which way to go, he took the road that seemed to be headed west, and soon it went from a narrow two lanes, to a wide two lanes, and he felt pretty good about his choice of roads until he heard the back left tire blow out.

But he didn't even know about Dave Olshaker.

Chapter Six

1

Now, back up a few days.

Back to the Saturday night when the rest of them all took off in the Pimpmobile for the West Coast. Picture a big strapping guy of twenty, in the back of a pickup truck, with eyes that just popped open like he'd come back from the dead. He'd had a dream, and it involved a couple of things he didn't like to think about, one of them being his friend Billy Dunne, and it freaked him out to think about it. Dave Olshaker snarfled awake, farting as he woke, and he was royally pissed. He'd been up 'til at least six or seven A.M., and after leaving Tammy in the frat house, he'd gotten in the pickup with his buddy Billy Dunne and gone to do 360s in the mud of the cow pasture out by McCrory's lake. Sometime, in a haze of beer and piss, he passed out. Woke up, looking at the back of Billy's head, too. What a shocker that had been.

It was like the dream! Just like the dream!

He didn't like to think about what happened the night before. Even if he could remember, which he wasn't so sure about, given the Mother of Hangovers that held him in its warm embrace. He had a taste of what he had come to think of as sour ass in his mouth, and a hammering in the head that so distracted him that he barely realized he'd woken up in the backseat of his Ford pickup truck.

He got on the road once he found out from one of Bronwyn Shapiro's friends exactly what route they were taking. He told her Bronwyn's dad had called, and he needed to call him back to let him know. "For safety."

And that's when a girl named Kathy Emmons stepped forward and told him how to track them down.

2

His head hurt so much, Olshaker ended up having to pull over at a place he liked to call Motel 69. Billy got the room, and Olshaker barely got his sorry ass to the bed before passing out again. Before he turned off the bedside light, he told Billy he had to sleep on the far side of the bed.

"Why?" Billy's eyes were all bloodshot and his face was pockmarked from too many Milky Way bars and Mr. Pibbs and Pabst Blue Ribbon in between to wash it all down. He looked like an old man with a mop of bright yellow hair thrown on his scalp.

" 'Cause you stink," Olshaker said, but it wasn't completely true. He was a little afraid that he'd start dreaming about Tammy and in the dream wrap his legs around her; only when he woke up, it might be Billy's thighs rubbing against him.

Out of this general fear, Olshaker kept his clothes on that night.

They'd lost a day, but they got back on the road and ended up pretty much following the route that the Pimpmobile had taken.

And he was there in Arizona when the Pimpmobile took the wrong turn off the main highway.

He drove his truck up to a plateau and got out binoculars to watch what Tammy was up to with her friends.

And when they got the flat tire, he turned to Billy Dunne and said, "Holy shit. We got 'em, buddy. We got 'em."

"What do we do now?"

Dave Olshaker thought a moment, cocking his head back to look up at the white blank sky. Then Dave reached down under his seat and drew out a warm can of Pabst, popped the top and took a chug down. "Kee-rist, I don't know. But that jock-strapped pretty boy has my baby. And I mean to get her back any way I can. She belongs to me."

3

"Son of a bitch!" Griff said. He had kicked the tire six or seven times as if he could bring it back to life.

"You really don't have a spare?" Bronwyn whispered to Josh, pressing her lips so close that he could feel her heat on top of the heat of the day.

Josh looked out over the highway. It was not the route they were supposed to take. Nothing but scrub and dust and a long barbed-wire fence that made him think somebody actually owned this corner of hell. Sweat trickled down his back, and he felt a mushiness of sweat around his balls, and he wished he had a nice motel room with a long cool shower.

Ziggy was already toking out on a big rock above the highway. "Hey, I see somebody coming!"

"Yeah?" Tammy shouted back.

"A trucker! We're gonna get a lift. I know we are!" He shot his arm out, pointing to the west. "There's something way over there, man! It looks like a gas station. All we have to do is get the trucker to give us a ride, and we're set."

"Thank God," Bronwyn said, lifting a cigarette in the air like she was flipping the bird. "This is my last smoke."

4

The truck was a big-ass Kenmore, and the guy slowed down, pulling on his horn. Tammy was out in the middle of the highway, jumping up and down. It was her tits that did it—that's what everyone felt without having to say a word about it. Someday, they'd build a memorial to her boobs. They were bouncing like basketballs, and no trucker in his right mind wouldn't have come to a stop just to see whether it was a mirage or a real live woman of twenty with humongous breasts.

"Men never cease to live down to my expectations," Bronwyn said, shaking her head. She dropped the last of her cigarette in the dust. She stubbed at it with her toe, then shivered a little as if she were cold.

"You okay?" Josh asked.

"Just that feeling. You know—the one where they say a goose walked over your grave. Like something's wrong." Then she laughed. "Maybe I just need another cigarette."

5

Bronwyn had to scrunch up next to the trucker, but she didn't mind. He was a rugged, rode-hard kind of guy with a face that must've been pretty at one time, but turned into baked granite from

57

the sun, with crack lines along his smile and around his eyes.

"Best I can do is dump you two up ahead. There's a place about two miles up."

"That'd be great," Josh said.

"It was nice of you to stop," Bronwyn said, then leaned a bit against his shoulder. He smelled like axle grease, but there was something comforting about it.

"I drive this highway eight times a week, back and forth. There ain't much here." He introduced himself: Ely. He told them about his life, which was mainly the road and a little shack out in a town called Naga, not too far away. You knew you had reached his place because a paved road ended where a dirt road shot off to the west, and you could see a silvery glimmer—from all the hubcaps hanging on the front fence and you could hear the music he blasted from his workshop out back. "Mainly ZZ Top. Mainly. Sometimes I get into the mood for Boston. But mainly ZZ."

"That's quite a life," Josh said.

"Ha," Ely spat back. "I bet you kids are rich and are on spring break and just tooling around because you got nothin' else to do."

"I think that pretty much sums it up, except we really don't have money," Bronwyn said. Glancing sidelong at Josh, cigarette hanging from her lips, "Don't you think?"

"Abso," he said.

"Abso?" Ely laughed when he heard the word.

"That's frat-boy talk for absolutely."

"Ha. Well, you get out here, kiddies, and life smacks you like you're the bug and it's the windshield. Ass first, and you got about two seconds to dodge."

"So what's this town like? Nada?"

"Naga. It's a little town. You'd hate it, rich boy," Ely said. "Jesus H, why even talk to you about it? You'll never go there. Look," Ely said, pointing toward a rise to the left—a long flat corrugated metal roof canopied gas pumps that looked like they were out of the 1920s. Behind it, a long rectangular building with a curved metal roof and three big signs with various versions of: SEE THE ATTRACTION! DON'T GO HOME WITHOUT SEEING THE ATTRACTION! THE UNSPEAKABLE UNKNOWABLE MYSTERY! IT'S THE EIGHTH WONDER OF THE WORLD AND THE SECOND WONDER OF THE NEW WORLD! 75 CENTS ADMISSION! BUY INDIAN BLANKETS! GET COFFEE! GAS IS CHEAP! COFFEE'S CHEAPER!

"Wow. It's where I wanted to go," Bronwyn said. "It's the Unspeakable Mystery place."

"They sound a little desperate," Josh said.

"I usually never stop here," Ely said.

"Why's that?" Josh asked.

"That thing they got. That attraction. Gives me the creeps."

Ely slowed the truck, and it groaned and rattled a bit. He turned the wheel to the left, crossing the empty highway, then turned the wheel to the right, taking the truck onto the gravel service road.

6

When he dropped them off near the pumps, Ely said, "Now, if you ever get lost out here, find your way over to Naga, and look for end of the paved road and the silvery light from the hubcaps in the sun and ZZ Top blasting from the back. You're welcome to see my place and check out Naga. It's a cool town, but probably not as sophisticated as you two. You kids be careful on the road. Lots of nuts out there."

7

The Brakedown Palace and Sundries was the biggest thing for miles—mainly because there was nothing around it. Bronwyn went in to buy some more cigarettes, and Josh went around by the garage bays to look for the boss.

A big man, the size of a bear and with a growl not far from one, rose out of a grease pit in the back. He had sun-baked copper skin that had begun to go from tan to alligator hide. "Whatja want?"

"Our car's got a flat. Just back a little ways. Down the road."

The man's eyes were almost like fish-eyes, nearly perfectly round. A nose like a hammer and big lips that held an unlit cigarette between them. He wore a black bandanna tied around his head, and an enormous white T-shirt clung tight to his barrel-chest and potbelly. His hips were wide, and his stained jeans looked like they were home-made. On his feet, boots with steel tips at the toes. He was exactly what Bronwyn would call "a real character."

"Hell, kid, I'm busy. You need a tow? It'll be twenty minutes at best."

"Okay," Josh said.

"Fifty bucks."

"Fifty? It's just a couple miles away. Fifty bucks?"

"Take it or leave it."

"I don't know. I just don't know. Fifty? Doesn't that seem a little absurd?"

The man shrugged, and then wiped some grease-sweat off his brow. "There's another gas station, twenty-five miles up. You want to go there, I ain't stoppin' you."

8

After a discussion with Bronwyn, the fee was paid, the tow truck went out, and soon enough, Tammy, Griff, and Ziggy showed up, looking as if they had been drained of all energy, with the car hooked like a mackerel to the back of the truck.

The big guy was named Charlie Goodrow, and after introducing himself around, he told them that they could each have a Coke on him.

"Fifty bucks worth of Coke," Josh said.

The sun was moving westward too fast, and someone finally asked Goodrow how long it might take for the tire change. Charlie Goodrow laughed and said, "Go wander the shop. I'll have it down in twenty minutes. Or less. I'll check your brakes, too. Free of charge."

"Fifty bucks worth of checking brakes," Josh said, only barely under his breath.

"I want to go see the Great Unspeakable Mystery," Bronwyn said. "It's less than a buck and you enter in the back of the store."

9

All of them went into the Sundries Shop for the free Cokes. Tammy wanted to look at the cheap jewelry they had near the Indian blankets. Bronwyn grabbed Griff by the elbow, and tugged him toward the back of the shop. There was a narrow door there, and it had a sign that read, *For the CHEAP ADMISSION PRICE of just 75 CENTS! See the Eighth Wonder of the World! The Mystery of the Southwest! The Aztec Demon Known as Xipe Totec! Found many miles south of here, smuggled up by an outlaw who believed it contained treasures! SEE THE UNSPEAKABLE SAVAGE MYSTERY OF THE ANCIENT PRE-COLUMBIAN WORLD!*

"Come on," Bronwyn said, pulling on his arm. Griff pulled away.

"I'm waiting for Tammy."

"Josh?" Bron let go of Griff, and stomped over to where Josh stood near the glass refrigerator, sipping his Coke.

"Okay, but we're not paying," Josh said. "We've already blown tonight's motel room budget on the car. I don't intend to make Charlie Goodrow a little richer."

10

Griff and Tammy followed them, and Ziggy showed up soon after, slurping his Coke through a straw. There was a little box for the quarters, but none of them put any in, and since it was honor system, they snuck through the entry feeling like delinquents. Josh didn't, though. He felt damn good when he went in there and said, "Fifty bucks worth of the Unspeakable Mystery of the Universe."

The corridor was dark, but with fine spears of light that came through at the roof's edge. They'd left the rectangular building of the Brakedown Palace and Sundries, and had entered on a concrete floor, down a walkway with corrugated metal walls and what seemed to be a curved roof.

"It's a Quonset hut," Josh said. "They had them on the sub base when I was a kid."

"Navy brat," Tammy said, in a way that was so sexy it nearly turned Josh on to hear her voice. She purred like a kitten sometimes.

The spears of light became brighter. Bulbs had been strung along the roof, hanging down like clunky Christmas ornaments. The wiring above their heads was exposed as the lights brightened.

"Jeez," Ziggy said. "This is like some freak show."

He pointed to the metal walls. Small dried animals hung by strings—lizards, rats, rabbits, quail.

"That's sick."

"It's just trash you find on the desert," Griff said. "Dried-up crap and dead animals."

As they ventured forward, they entered a well-lit space that had a poorly made wood and stone sculpture. "The ancient Aztecs were a fierce, bloodthirsty people," Bronwyn read from the sign above the sculpture. "Jesus, some moron wrote this up. Ignorant desert scum." She glanced at the diorama. "Oh my God, look," she said with a voice that seemed filled with childish wonder yet still held the possibility of being disgusted. "They're little Aztecs, sacrificing someone. How adorable. And repulsive."

Josh crouched down and glanced over the divider that kept the diorama and sculpture protected from tourists. "That's funky." It was a replica of a Mexican pyramid, about knee high, and at the flat top, a little stone-carved man was cutting open another little stone-carved man. On the wall, beyond this, a cheap plastic replica of a Mayan calendar. "Someone's obsessed with Aztecs and Mayans here."

"Some redneck who doesn't know his history well enough," Bronwyn said.

"It's like a dollhouse of death," Tammy said, a sweet edge to her voice.

"You're my doll," Griff said, pulling her tightly into him, and somehow managing to unbutton the top two buttons of her blouse at the same time.

They moved on, down the long corridor that went alternately dark and then light again as various kinds of bulbs and lamps lit sections, highlighting pictures that had obviously been torn from a book on the Aztecs. There was a scene of blood running from a warrior's chest, a look of horror on his face, as several priests stood around him, with one raising his still-beating heart high. Other large pictures included a poorly done painting of what appeared to be a tomb with stone jaguars and scorpions and what Josh guessed was the Aztec god, Quetzalcoatl. A crystal skull hung suspended above their heads. They all giggled and snorted or just laughed out loud as they passed through a spotlighted area with a tall wooden sculpture of a naked woman. The sign behind the sculpture read, *This work of art was found behind the arroyo and is believed to have been carved by the Ancients.*

Finally, a new doorway, and over it, the sign, *It's not too late to turn back! You don't want to see the Unspeakable Mystery! The Ancient Savage Flayer of Men! The Flesh-Scraper of the Pyramids of Teotihuacán!*

Josh was the first one through the door, and what he saw there made him cry out.

PART TWO

THE UNSPEAKABLE

Chapter Seven

1

Dave Olshaker had been on the road too long, and he was sleepy as hell. He and Billy Dunne had to slap each other a few times just to keep their eyes open, and then the heat of the day just fried them out, that and the warm piss beer. Dave had to take a dump twice back in the sagebrush because something he'd eaten the night before hadn't set well.

But they had watched it all.

Billy had wanted to go help with the tire change. "It's our chance. We can help 'em, then beat the crap out of Griff. And you can get Tammy."

But Dave, not feeling so great, had held back. He'd just driven around and around the narrow, dusty side road off the highway, trying to keep out of sight of the gang with the Pimpmobile.

Once the tow truck had come out, he decided to follow it up to the Brakedown Palace, but he still stayed a ways back until he saw all of them go inside the shop.

When he drove up to the Palace, he gassed up the car, then went inside.

"Fuel," Billy said, grabbing Hostess Cupcakes, Twinkies, and some Drake's Yodels from the shelves, stuffing them down his pants as if the bulge wouldn't be noticeable.

"That a Twinkie in your jeans, or are you just happy to see me?" Dave chuckled.

"Where'd they go anyway?" Billy asked.

Charlie Goodrow had come back inside the shop, and pointed to the doorway in the back. "They went back there. And you're paying for every damn Twinkie you got in your pants, kid."

2

Inside the inner sanctum, Josh was shocked by the smell—it was of some kind of church incense. The room was smoky with it.

The others came up behind him, Tammy coughing, Ziggy saying something about getting high off "sacred fumes," and Bronwyn pointing out the lack of ventilation, despite the cigarette hanging out of her mouth.

But Josh had already gone over to the display case. The Mystery. The Great and Powerful It.

With spotlights on signs and images behind it—signs that warned of ancient curses and Aztec savagery, and images of the Pyramids of the Sun and Moon as well as of some man-creature covered with blood, holding what looked like a human head in his hands—a glass case stood at the center of the room, lit from beneath and behind with a cool blue and white light, and within the glass display, some kind of curved rock.

It was in what looked like a large stone bowl. As if a geode the size of a desk had been cracked open to cradle it.

"It's a dead kid," Griff said.

"No, it's not. Look at the hands."

"And feet," Josh added. "Christ."

"It's disgusting," Tammy said.

"I don't know," Bronwyn said. "Makes me feel a little creepy. But it has its good points."

"Like?"

Bronwyn shrugged. "It looks like the kind of baby someone I know will have someday."

"Like a baby freak," Griff said.

The only one not talking much was Ziggy. Josh noticed that he just stood off to the side, and wouldn't do more than peer at the Great Unspeakable Mystery from the corner of his eye, as if it reminded him of something not so wonderful.

The thing itself was a light dusty gray color all over with a sort of brackish, almost seaweed under-color to it—faint but noticeable. Its skull seemed enlarged, as if it were too big for the rest of its skeleton. Wrapped around its head and along its collarbone were gauzelike strips that criss-crossed all the way to its shriveled belly. Its skin was somehow glued to the gauze, and Josh blurted out, "It's a mummy. A creepy little crappy mummy. These people are whack jobs to sell tickets to it."

Its hands were elongated, with fingers that looked more like fins that then curled into talons. At the end of its fingertips, what looked like long, sharp, curved, black, shiny, smooth stone that ended in hooks. Its feet and toenails were similar.

In its eye sockets, two rounded turquoise stones in place of eyes.

Bronwyn read aloud from one of the signs. "It is a creature of the night, although it never sleeps. But the Sun God is its enemy, and so it prefers darkness."

Its hands were crossed over each other, with a twisted, knotted rope keeping them together.

"It looks like a big baby, sleeping," Tammy cooed. "From hell."

"Big ugly bondage baby," Griff chuckled.

"It's the size of a kid. Maybe it's a small adult. I can't tell," Bronwyn said.

"I like the turquoise," Tammy added. "I kept hoping we'd find someplace that had decent jewelry out here. So far, this is the closest I've come to any."

"Maybe I should pop his little eyes out," Griff said. "Put them in a necklace for you."

"Ew," Tammy said.

"How could they do this?" Josh asked. "They

had to dig up a grave and then do something to the body? It's sick."

Bronwyn lit up a cigarette. "Maybe. But you know, out here on the desert, people die, bodies are found years later. The desert mummifies them. Maybe it's fake. I mean, it could be plastic."

"I bet it is," Griff said.

"Nope, it's real," Josh said.

"No way. Look at those hands. Nobody can have hands like that. Look at them. It's so fake it's funny."

Josh leaned over the glass cover of the display. "I can't tell. This is probably all fake."

"Just lift the lid up," Griff said. Then, he pushed Josh back a little and went to feel under the glass lid. "Here's the hinge." He raised the lid and held it back. "Touch it."

"No thanks."

"Oh Lord." Griff reached in and touched the forehead of the skull.

For just a second, Josh felt as if something happened. Not anything awful, just as if something changed. Then he began coughing. It was dust— the dust of the display case had come up in a brief smoky cloud and then dissipated.

"Hell," Griff said.

"What is it?"

"It's warm. This thing is warm."

"I'm sure," Bronwyn said. "It probably bakes in here every day."

"No, I mean, it's . . . it's . . . alive!" Griff shouted

and then cackled gleefully. Then, stupidly, he let go of the glass display top, and it fell backward, shattering on the floor.

Each of them looked at the other.

"I wonder how much that'll cost to replace," Bronwyn said.

After several seconds, Josh said, "They didn't hear it in the shop. We're too far out here."

"Well, we can't leave it like that."

"Oh yeah we can," Griff said.

That's when Josh noticed the sign. He read it aloud. "Please Do Not Touch Glass. We at the Brakedown Palace have nicknamed this special ancient mummy Scratch, and he has been good luck for us all these years. We must warn any who view it that there is a legend that once Scratch gets fresh human skin under its fingernails and the taste of blood, he'll come back from oblivion to reap the human harvest. Do Not Touch. Do Not Feed."

"Scratch. Now that's original," Bronwyn said. "That's nothing but some little kid mummified and they stuck fake longer fingernails on him. But they call him Scratch. Lovely Mr. Goodrow."

"There's something wrong with this," Tammy said. For the first time since he'd known her, Josh felt he heard something adult in her voice, as if she'd been hiding behind a little-girl persona during college. "I don't feel good about it."

"I know. It's not right," Ziggy said, startling the others.

Josh turned—Ziggy had pressed himself up against the metal wall. He was tripping somehow—it looked as if he'd finally hit the legendary limit of too much weed and too much speed. "What's up? Zig?"

"I had a dream about this. A vision. Like a shaman."

Griff snorted. "Doin' 'shrooms, was ya?"

"I had this vision where I saw this thing coming for me, only it was all bloody and torn up, but it had eyes just like this."

"It was a dream. That's all," Josh said.

"I don't know. I am never ever taking anything again," Ziggy said. "Crap. My brain is fried. I know it is."

Bronwyn went over to him and touched the edge of his elbow. "It's okay. It's okay. Look, let's go back down to the shop. I'm sure the car's nearly ready. We can get some Cokes. Want a Coke? My treat."

"Some freak put this together," Ziggy whispered. "Some freak. Some sick nutjob. That's a kid. Or a dwarf. Or a very little person. Jesus Holy Mother of Mary."

"It's okay," Bronwyn said, softly. She tugged at his arm, and Ziggy, head down, began walking with her down the long corridor, past the paintings and the stonework of the Quonset hut, back to the shop at the Brakedown Palace.

"I never wanna get that burnt out on drugs," Tammy said. "I like weed too much."

"Remember that acid?"

75

"Only three times," Tammy said.

"Let's get out of here," Josh said.

"Eh, we just broke some cheap piece of glass. It's no biggie," Griff said. "Hey, let's find out if this thing is real. Let's feed it."

"Hardy-har-har."

"I mean it. Come on. We can just give it a little skin. Just a little."

"You're getting creepy on me, baby," Tammy said.

"Creepy can be good." Griff reached for her left breast and gave it a squeeze. Tammy slapped him hard on the cheek—the smack echoed as much as the breaking glass had.

Josh stood there, wishing he could disappear.

"You slut," Griff spat, and swung a fist out at Tammy, connecting with the side of her neck. Tammy fell—knocked off her feet by the blow.

"Hey!" Josh moved forward, grabbing Griff's arm, pulling it back. Griff tugged hard, pulling Josh off balance. "Leave me the hell alone!" Griff shouted. Josh wasn't sure what he yelled back, and he was only dimly aware that Tammy was screaming and weeping in a heap in the corner, but the next thing he knew, he was thrown backward into the glass display case. He felt a sliver of glass go into his side, then a sick little crunch. At first, he thought he'd broken his back, but then realized it was just the Unspeakable Mystery Attraction, Scratch, beneath him.

Josh started cussing, and when he was done, whispered, "You probably killed me."

Griff's face was deep red and sweaty—but the smash-up of the display had gotten his attention and stopped the fight.

"*Did* I kill you?" Griff asked.

Griff gingerly pulled Josh up by the waist from the broken display.

Josh felt a pain in his back and side, but after a minute, lifting his torn shirt up, Griff only found two small bits of glass, and they had just scraped his skin a bit.

"Oh man," Griff said.

"You are one fat moron," Tammy said, as if it were the worst insult she could hurl.

"Okay. Just leave me alone," Josh said, pulling back from Griff.

"I want to make sure you're okay."

"I'm fine. Okay? I'm fine. Don't touch me. And do not hit her ever again."

"She hit me first," Griff said.

"What, are you two years old? She slapped you because you copped a feel. And you slugged her. Get a grip. See a psychiatrist. But don't ever hit her again."

Then, to Tammy, "You okay?"

She rubbed her neck and accepted his outstretched hand as a lift up. "I'm fine."

"Oh baby, I'm sorry," Griff said. "I'm so sorry, baby."

"I know you are." Tammy let go of Josh's hand and stepped toward Griff.

I do not believe this, Josh thought. *They are going to kiss and make up.*

And that's when he happened to glance down and see the smashed-up body of Scratch.

"We broke it. Holy mother of—"

"Damn it to hell!" a gruff voice shouted from down the corridor.

Josh spun around—it was none other than Charlie Goodrow with a big shotgun at his side.

Chapter Eight

1

One of them shrieked; another shouted a brief but potent profanity; and still another gasped. Josh wasn't even sure who'd shouted—it might've even come from his mouth. They all went running—at least that's what it seemed like—Josh pushing Bronwyn forward through the final door that expelled them into blinding sunlight. They ran as fast as they could to the car, which was parked just outside the garage bay at the side of the Brakedown Palace Gas and Sundries building. Josh noticed that the gas cap was off, but that didn't matter. They had to get the hell out of there.

"Where's Griff?" Tammy cried out, alternately laughing hysterically and whining a bit.

"Just get in!" Josh said, shoving her into the back of the car. Ziggy, somehow, had already managed to squeeze into the back ahead of them.

"Hurry up! He's crazy!" Bronwyn shouted from the front seat.

Then there was the sound of the shotgun's blast.

"Griff!" Bronwyn shouted.

But Griff came running around the corner with what looked like a kid in his arms. He was laughing hysterically as he ran.

"Go! Go!" he shouted and then leapt into the shotgun seat of the car, squeezing Bronwyn over into Josh's driver's seat. Josh got the car in reverse, and his foot dropped heavily onto the accelerator. The car screeched, and then he tried to put it in drive, but it went in neutral instead. The thought flashed through his mind that the engine would stall, but he knocked the lever into drive, and at that moment, here's what he saw, frozen in some strange tableau, as if he'd set off a flash camera to stop the action of life for a moment:

Not Charlie Goodrow running from the back of the Palace, but someone who looked big and slovenly and had a little blond sidekick with him. It registered who it was:

Dave Olshaker? What the—

Then the action of life began again, and Dave limped and half-jogged toward them. "I been shot!" Dave shouted, clutching his ass. "I been shot!"

"Sons of bitches!" his sidekick shouted at them.

"Tammy! I love you, baby! Come back to me!"

Dave howled, then fell to the pavement, his hands still nursing his butt.

But the Pimpmobile was already heading out onto the service road, kicking up dust and gravel in its wake.

2

"This is just too much to process," Bronwyn said when Josh finally slowed the car down, having driven off the road a little and out behind a hill at least twenty miles away from the Brakedown Palace.

"What the hell was Olshaker doing? What the hell?" Josh asked, glancing in the rearview mirror at Tammy, who glared back at him.

"Don't look at me," she said. "I dumped him a long time ago. I guess some people just never give up."

"He's a prick," Griff said. "But looks like he got shot up in the hiney."

Sometime between spinning out of the gas station and getting out onto the dusty road, Josh had realized what Griff had brought with him.

The Unspeakable Scratch.

"Little bastard," as Ziggy started to call it.

"You stole that thing?"

"Come on. It's not just a thing. It's the Unspeakable Mystery of the Ancient Aztecs," Griff said, holding his prize up on his lap, like a ventriloquist's dummy. "Hello, my name is Scratch."

"I gotta pee," Tammy said. "Come on. I gotta pee. When I get nervous, I gotta pee."

"Okay, okay," Bronwyn said. "Get out and go take a leak."

"Come with me. I'm scared."

Bronwyn made a noise of moderate disgust from the back of her throat, but flicked her cigarette out into the dirt and pushed Griff and his stolen Mystery out of the car. "What, are you two years old?" she asked Tammy.

"There might be snakes. And scorpions."

"One can only hope," Bronwyn said.

3

"What happened back there?"

"It was funny as hell," Griff said. "That old man came at us with the gun, but he didn't know that Olshaker and his buddy were right behind him. God knows what the hell Olshaker's doing out here. He's obsessed with my girl, and I guess he's been trailing us. Well, the old guy spun around, Olshaker squealed like a little kid and tried to grab the shotgun. I was surprised to see the little creep myself, but after you guys took off, you missed the best part—Olshaker and his buddy were fighting with the old guy for the shotgun, and I just saw this little fella and decided he'd be great back at The House." Griff always referred to his frat house as The House. Scratch would not be the first thing he'd ever stolen for The House. He had a stag's head from one of the dean's homes up in the balcony room on the second floor, and he'd even stolen a trophy from a rival football team and they had it in the basement of The House. "Imagine this little guy up on the mantel during a party. Cowabunga!" He laughed, pulling the little mummy's arms up in the air, pretending to talk with a babyish voice. "I'm the Monster of The House! Wheee!"

"Why'd you steal it?"

He shrugged. "Chill out. He's all broke up around the ribs. We'd have had to pay for it anyway." Then, he held up one of Scratch's fingernails. "See? Broke right off." He passed it over to Josh, who nearly pricked his finger on the sharp tip.

"It's obsidian. Like a knife. Sharp as hell."

"I think it's a cool souvenir from this crappy trip," Griff said.

Ziggy in the backseat had already lit a joint, and he and Griff passed it back and forth, waiting for the girls to come back to the car.

They were all quiet for a minute or two, and then Ziggy said, "Just don't feed that little bastard."

"Huh?"

"I said don't feed it."

"I wonder what it eats," Griff said. "I mean, if it eats skin or blood, then I hate to say it, but our buddy Josh already gave it its first meal. Look." Griff pressed his finger to Scratch's clenched jaws. He drew his finger back and held it up. A tiny spot of blood. "When you fell on it, buddy. It got a little taste o' Joshua."

"We're so very, very screwed," Ziggy said.

4

"Don't be ridiculous," Josh laughed. "Oh my God, Ziggy, give up the weed. It's messing with your head. I mean it. Give it up."

"No, we're cursed. I know we are. That little bastard was in my vision dream. Shamans used mushrooms and herbs and weed to see things. I saw it. I had a shaman trip. I saw the little bastard in it. We're up shit's creek like nobody's ever been up shit's creek."

"Further up the creek than you'd guess, plowboy," Griff said. He pointed to the gas gauge.

It was just beneath empty.

"Great. Just great," Josh said, hitting the horn with his fist.

The sound of the horn echoed across the dusty road.

5

After a minute, Ziggy said, "Throw the little bastard out. It's bad luck."

6

The trunk of the Pimpmobile popped up.

"This is the ugliest, nastiest thing I've ever seen," Josh said. "When we get going again, we're going to return it. We are."

"No way," Griff said, heaving Scratch into the back of the trunk, among the girls' suitcases and the guys' backpacks and clothes.

They both stared at it.

"What were you thinking? What was going on in that mind of yours? You thought, 'I'll add robbery to my college career. Not just robbery, but stealing a nasty stupid sick little gas station mummy that's probably covered with some diseased lice or something.' "

"Look. Live slow, die slow if you want. I watched my grampa live like that and he ended up spending ten years in a damn nursing home. You live like that, you get a long, boring life. Go ahead. Have that life. Someday when you're in that nursing home sucking back puree and poopin' your diapers, you're going to remember this moment," Griff said, chuckling. "You'll remember its face. Look at it. With its little grin. It's kinda cute."

"That's not a grin. That's dried-up flesh around clenched teeth in some old corpse with an enlarged skull. That is the ugliest thing I've ever seen."

"Don't say that about my newborn baby. It's

grinning," Griff said, then slammed the trunk closed. He slapped his hand around Josh's shoulder. "It does not get cooler than this."

"You just put a corpse in with my clothes," Josh said.

"Don't think of it as a corpse. Think of it," Griff said, "as a memento."

7

Tammy dropped trou and stepped out of her panties to squat down and take a leak.

"You okay?" Bronwyn asked, her back to Tammy.

"Fine."

"Olshaker must really love you," Bronwyn said.

"Like a bounty hunter," Tammy said. When she was done, she got back into her panties and jeans, zipping up. "He's a guy I'd like to put in jail."

"He steal something of yours?"

"Maybe," Tammy said. "You got a smoke on you?"

"Sure," Bron said. "Here ya go." She passed her one of the few remaining cigarettes. Then, she slid one out of the pack for herself and lit it up. Sucked in that first taste of smoke. "I know I'm going to have to quit someday. Everybody either quits or gets cancer."

"Or both," Tammy said, lighting hers from Bronwyn's.

"When I'm having a bad day, a smoke just takes the edge off things."

"How true. I started when I was fourteen because I saw an ad with these beautiful women smoking and I wanted to be one of them. Stupid, huh? But I was fourteen and I didn't look like much then and I just wanted to be grown up more than anything in the world." Tammy blew a perfect smoke ring into the air.

"I started smoking when my folks split. I was a little younger than that. I thought I was intellectual to do it. I thought all these French intellectuals smoke," Bronwyn laughed, coughing out a brief white cloud. "I think that's pretty stupid, too. I snuck cigarettes from my mother's purse. She didn't smoke much, so she always had a full pack. She never mentioned the ones that were missing."

"We have a lot in common." Tammy grinned. "I snuck smokes from my older brother's sock drawer. They always smelled a little like dirty feet because he rarely ever washed his gym socks. He just balled them up and threw them in there on top of his packs of Marlboros."

Bronwyn let out a guffaw. "I had a boyfriend once who never washed anything. He smelled like a locker room half the time."

They both puffed on their cigarettes.

Tammy said, softly, "You still love Griff."

Bronwyn took a breath. "Yeah, I guess I do. I guess I do." She glanced over at Tammy and chuckled slightly. "It's stupid, I know. I'm practically the top of our class, I'm planning to get a master's and then maybe even a Ph.D., and he probably wants the kind of woman who . . ." Realizing what she'd just begun saying, she added, "I don't mean . . . what it sounds like . . . I mean . . . I mean, what I mean—"

Tammy cut her off. "I know how you think of me. I know what the other girls think, too. But what you don't know about me could fill a book. But I know what you mean."

"I'm a jerk," Bronwyn said.

"I like him," Tammy said. "But he's not the kind of guy you're really supposed to fall in love with."

The sky was beautiful and Bronwyn's eyes started filling with tears, which she quickly wiped away.

Tammy slung an arm over Bronwyn's shoulder. "You should find someone new. He's not the best guy. He's a fun guy. But he's not right for you. Or for me. We're gonna break up."

"What? You have all this . . . sex all the time."

"Sure," Tammy said, puffing on the cig. "I like sex with him. He likes sex with me. But there's not much else."

"Oh."

"Yeah, I know what that 'oh' means. 'Oh, you're happy being a slut.' Just because I like to party and have a little fun, doesn't mean I'm just some mindless bimbo. Look, we're in college. Someday I'm going to be like my mother. I know it. I can feel it. All uptight and full of rules and making sure the silver's polished for Thanksgiving, even if I have some half-assed career. I know I'm headed that way. And I want to put that off as long as possible. I don't want to get an M.R.S. degree. I don't want a ring on my finger, not yet. Not for years. And Griff is . . . Griff is a pretty boy. He's a jock. He's a guy who's young and has fun and gets along with nearly everybody when he's not acting like a four-year-old. He's not long-term for me. Or for you."

"Says you."

"That's right," Tammy said. "Says me."

"You don't think you might be hurting yourself?" Bronwyn asked.

Tammy drew back a little and began walking to the car. She turned around to glance at Bronwyn, after just a few steps forward. "You might just ask yourself that same question."

8

After the girls got back, they all piled back into the Pimpmobile. Josh drove another few miles along the road, but finally the car came to a sputtering halt.

"End of the line," Ziggy said. "Nowheresville, USA."

Josh felt a pain in his stomach—a knot of tension. "You know, you'd think I'd be smart enough to fill up with gas at a gas station."

"I didn't think it was near empty," Griff said. "I'm almost positive we had half a tank left."

"Almost," Tammy said, somewhat archly.

Bronwyn said, "It's nearly six. I wonder what time it'll get dark."

"We've got food in the back," Griff said. "We still have the cooler full of beer, too."

"And a mummified body stolen from a gas station," Josh said. "Or did you forget that? Will the beer taste better with a little corpse on it?" He slapped his forehead. "Christ Almighty! My dad told me to get a CB radio in case I ever got stuck somewhere. He told me. He said, 'Josh, you never know when the car's going to break down.' He doesn't really give a flyer about me most of the time, but this was one of those few times when he did," Josh said, slowly, softly. "I'm so stupid. Stupid. Stupid."

"I wonder if the guy at the Brakedown Palace is calling the cops," Ziggy said. "We stole his big attraction."

"That piece of crap?" Griff snorted. "He'll dig up another corpse in some old Indian graveyard around here. It's just one of a thousand out there. He probably puts a new one in every year."

9

Somewhere nearby, in some dark, nearly airless place, a breath was exhaled, and motes of dust and nearly microscopic bits of bone coughed from a jaw that had not opened in a long, long time.

Chapter Nine

1

They made a fire in the dirt. Bronwyn's lighter had come in handy. Josh and Griff gathered some slender sticks of wood for kindling, and then a larger piece of some dried-up gray wood that burned really well. They spread a couple of thin cotton blankets out on the ground and spent some time making sure there weren't any creepy-crawlies nearby.

They passed around the contents of the bag of junk food that Bronwyn had bought at the Brakedown Palace. Gas station sandwiches, Tastee-Cakes, and a couple of warm Cokes passed around like it was Holy Communion wine.

The beer was cool, and they each got a can. Suddenly, as the sun went down in a blaze of pink and gold glory, Josh felt pretty good.

"This is an adventure," he said, leaning back against Bronwyn's knees.

"Some adventure," she said.

"Nope, he's right," Griff said. "My uncle told me to have a lot of adventures in college. This could be cool."

"When we're completely dried up and burning up in the sun, we won't call this an adventure," Bronwyn said. "We'll call it the last day of our life. And I'm never making it to L.A. I can tell you that."

"You're kidding, right?" Tammy asked. "We're not in any real trouble here. I don't think."

Bronwyn shrugged. "Okay. I guess I was exaggerating. I have three packs of Merits left, so I'll live."

"Until the cigs kill you," Griff said.

"Years from now I'll regret smoking. But right now, I regret nothing, as they say."

Ziggy kept looking out in the purple darkness. "I wonder if there are wolves."

"There aren't wolves," Josh said. "I don't think. Maybe coyotes. But we don't have to worry about them."

"Yeah, coyotes, rattlesnakes, big black scorpions the size of my wang," Griff said.

Josh made a sound in the back of his throat.

Griff shot him a look. "Yeah?"

"Your wang always seems to come up, if you'll pardon the expression."

Griff grinned. "He needs a breath of fresh air now and then."

"Yuck." Bronwyn coughed.

Tammy laughed. "Oh, good grief, get a sense of humor, you guys. Hey, this is like Girl Scout camp."

"Time to make a few brownies, then," Griff said, heading off into the darkness to do his business.

Bron and Josh both groaned at his gross joke.

"Damn, that reminds me," Bronwyn said. "Anybody bring toilet paper?"

"I have a ton of tissues in my backpack," Tammy said. "In the trunk."

"Good. I hope it's a ton that will last all of us through tomorrow. Damn. I wonder how far it is to the nearest town."

"Hey!" Josh said, leaning forward and sitting up. "Naga. That was the name of the town. We can't be more than, I don't know, ten, fifteen miles. It was on the map."

"The map you lost?"

"I didn't lose it. It fell out of my back pocket. I guess when I fell on that little bastard." He grinned, glancing at Ziggy who kept his eyes on the fire.

"If this town is that close, why can't we see it?" Griff asked from a distance. "I mean, I don't see lights anywhere out there."

"I bet it's north of here. I bet we're south of where we thought we were. I bet it's over those hills," Josh pointed up to the ridge of hills that seemed to have an aura of indigo against the ever-dimming sky.

"Maybe other cars will come by. Or truckers."

"Like Ely," Bronwyn said, remembering the truck driver who'd given them a lift.

"Yeah, you guys were lucky. He was cute," Tammy said.

"He was not cute," Griff said, coming back into the campfire circle. "He was a redneck."

"I hope you washed your hands," Tammy said.

"With sand." Griff grinned.

"Nope, Ely is high on the lustometer," Bronwyn said.

"God, I'm all out of brewsky," Griff finished the last of his beer.

"Lustometer?"

"Yep. Some guys are high on it."

"You got some weed to share, Zig?" Griff asked.

"I thought we said no pot," Josh said.

"Ziggy broke that rule at least two thousand miles ago. I bet you scored some in El Paso. Did you, Zig?"

Ziggy grinned. "Maybe. Maybe in Oklahoma."

"Oklahoma? They grow weed in Oklahoma?"

"Maybe somewhere along the road. We stopped in a lot of places. I ain't sayin'."

"I knew it!" Griff laughed, clapping his hands together. "Come on. We're all screwed here. Might as well enjoy it."

"I'm not into grass," Josh said.

"Tight-ass," Griff said.

"You don't have to smoke it," Bronwyn said. "Just make sure none of us gets too happy."

They all got high. Josh eventually joined in, and kept saying, "I don't think this is right. I'm only doing it because of peer pressure," and he felt guilty about smoking dope and wondered if the cops were going to descend and arrest them all.

"I got a joke," Griff said. "Here's how it goes."

"You're awful with jokes!" Bronwyn shouted.

"He's great at telling jokes. I love his jokes," Tammy said. "Tell it. Tell a good one, Griff."

"Okay. It is really, really good."

"So you say," Josh said.

"Okay. This guy goes into a restaurant. And the waitress, who is this hot little number with big tits and this great ass, says, 'What can I get you?' And the guy says, 'How about a quickie?' And the waitress says, 'You don't mean that. You mean—'"

Josh laughed, clapping his hands. "You're telling it all wrong. You're gonna give away the punchline."

Griff laughed. "Maybe I remembered it wrong."

"Okay, it's a stupid joke. It's really stupid," Josh said.

"Just let him tell it," Tammy said.

"No, I probably ruined it. You tell it," Griff said to Josh.

"Okay. But it's bad. Remember. It's bad and it's

stupid. Okay. A guy walks into a restaurant. He sits down. The waitress comes over and says, 'What're you having?' He says, 'How about a quickie?' And the waitress slaps him. Then she says, 'So tell me what you want, and none of this fresh stuff.' And he says, 'Well, I really want a quickie. I've never had one.' She slaps him again and stomps off. And the guy across from him, he's been watching this and he leans over and says to the guy, 'It's pronounced quiche.'"

No one laughed.

"I told you it was bad."

"Man, you cannot tell a joke!" Griff laughed. "Man, you just can't." And he started butchering yet another joke.

Sometime around midnight, after they'd laughed at several nearly nonexistent jokes, and the girls had gotten them singing "Michael, Row the Boat Ashore," and "Kumbaya," and then, "Let It Be," Ziggy passed out on the blanket in front of the fire, and Bronwyn began talking about her plans for the future, while Griff and Tammy went off into the darkness in their too-often mating ritual.

Josh, less stoned than the others, was the first to hear the noise from the car.

PART THREE

THE HUNTED

Chapter Ten

1

"What was that?"

"What?" Bronwyn asked sleepily, her eyes barely fluttering open.

"That noise."

"Probably a coyote. Don't worry," she said. "They don't get close to the fire."

"That was not a coyote," Josh said.

The noise got louder.

"That's metal."

She sat up on her elbows. "Maybe. I don't know. Maybe it's something kinky that Griff and Tammy are doing."

"That was the scrape of metal, Bron. It came from over there." Josh pointed toward the Pimp-mobile. He noticed just how far away they were from the road. To get to the car would take more than a minute. For some reason, this bothered him. It wasn't exactly a quarter mile away, but the car was far enough off in the darkness that it bothered him.

As if he had never been passed out at all, Ziggy sat straight up so fast that it freaked Josh out.

"It's that little bastard."

"What?"

"Ziggy, don't be silly," Bronwyn said. "You're high. We're all a little stoned."

"Maybe," Josh said, weighing this as a possibility. He sniffed the air. It had a curious mix of the dusty road and mesquite to it. But there was something else. Something that reminded him of a church smell. He wasn't sure what that was, but he assumed it was in his head. All of it, in his head.

"I didn't hear anything," Bronwyn said. But she said it as if she were trying to deny something even to herself. "I mean, I heard something. Just not something that seemed strange. I bet it's because those two are going at it. They're probably breaking the seats. They're going at it in your car."

"I don't think so," Ziggy said. "It's that little bastard. That's what it is. It's that little rat bastard."

Bronwyn pulled her knees into her chest and looked at the fire. She puffed away at her cigarette, and didn't seem bothered by the noise. *It's because she doesn't want to think about them,* Josh thought. *She doesn't want to think about Griff screwing Tammy. She loves Griff. There's no way around this. He hits girls. He's stupid. But he looks good and girls want that. They want to feel they got the football hero. They want to feel like they won some prize. Just like guys want pretty girls, no matter what the girl is on the inside.*

She's never going to look at me the way she looks at him. And he's a complete jerk. But she doesn't notice that. She just knows she wants him.

He scootched over in the dirt and sat next to her, crossing his legs in front of him. "You okay?" he asked.

She shrugged, holding her cigarette aloft as if she could write in the sky with it. "Life just sucks, that's all."

"I'm here," he said, looking at her, trying to make her see him. Really see him.

She turned her face toward him, and had an inscrutable look. "Don't cozy up to me if you just want something from me."

Ziggy pushed himself up from the rock on the other side of the fire. He stood there, beyond the crackling flame, a blanket wrapped around his shoulders. "What if it's all true? What if we brought that thing to life?" He balanced his weight on one foot and then the other, and looked toward the car nervously. "It's dark over there. I can't see anything. But I heard that."

"Sit down, Zig," Bronwyn said. "It's okay. You're freaking me out. Just calm down, have a smoke or something. I promise you that Scratchy-poo isn't coming out of that trunk."

Josh laughed. "Scratchy-poo."

"Scratchy-poo," Ziggy repeated, but didn't

laugh. He just kept watch in the direction of the car. "You know, I heard that sometimes these things have special powers. I mean, there are stones in England that Druids put together and they have ceremonies there still. And there's a place in France where there are these caves and they found these bones. It was some ancient religious thing. And I saw on *National Geographic* about this temple in India where there's this cult . . ."

"Zig," Bronwyn said. "What's your point?"

He looked at her, and the flickering from the firelight cast his face in a brilliant yellow and red shadow. "People believe in things. They do. And maybe if they believe in them bad enough, maybe those things can be real when they don't seem like they should."

"We should never have dragged you to *Texas Chainsaw Massacre* at Halloween," she said. Turning to Josh, "He screamed like a baby the whole time."

"You never know what stuff is like until it happens to you," Ziggy said. "You never know. People go missing all the time. Bad things happen to people and no one can explain them. I heard in Oregon that two kids got lost in the woods and got torn up, and they thought it was a tiger only no one could see how tigers could be in Oregon."

Bronwyn raised her hand. "Oh, pick me. I know! I know!"

Josh cracked up, laughing.

"What's so funny? It happened. They said the woods were cursed. They got torn up," Ziggy said.

"Zig, it was because of marijuana farms. That same weed you smoke doesn't come from nice Midwestern farmers. Some of them use tigers and mountain lions on their property to scare off—or kill—intruders."

Ziggy looked at the joint in his hand.

"What, you think marijuana is grown by Old MacDonald? That the Feds don't raid the plantations in Hawaii and the Northwest? That nice people run them and everybody's stoned and happy? They're drug lords, Zig. You smoke that stuff—hell, so do I now and then—and we're ultimately supporting people who would be happy to cut our throats if we stole an ounce of their stash. I know about those kids. I read about it. They were hiking where they shouldn't have gone hiking," she said.

"You know everything, don't you?" Ziggy said, an edge to his voice that wasn't quite sarcasm but close to it. "You know everything. Well, maybe we've gone where we shouldn't go hiking. I saw that thing. It's a sacred relic. I believe someone at that gas station stole it from where it was meant to rest. It's from some old religion that we can't even begin to understand. I believe people used to believe in it. And they died because of it. They laid down their lives in sacrifice. It freaks me out. It does. I think we're like those kids in the woods, off the path. And that thing is a tiger. Maybe a sleeping tiger. But sleeping tigers wake up. And when they wake up, they get hungry."

"Sit down," Bronwyn said. "It's the two sex fiends doing the nasty in the Pimpmobile."

2

Griff and Tammy hadn't made their way to the car until after they'd been up against a big flat rock that they'd stumbled across in the dark. Griff had his shirt off fast, and then was unbuttoning his shorts, which dropped to his ankles and he did what Tammy called his "penguin walk" over to her and nearly tore her top off to get to her breasts. Their lips locked, with tongues tickling, and Tammy kept whispering things to him when they weren't kissing, and it all turned him on more. She had left the condoms in the backseat of the Pimpmobile, and so she had to disengage. "I'm all dirty," she said.

"I feel that way, too," he said, grabbing around her back to keep his fingers on the nipples of delight, but she peeled his fingers back.

"I mean dirty dirty," she said. "All this damn sand. Now let go for a sec. I do not intend to get pregnant just yet and unless we just fool around, that's a distinct possibility." She jogged to the car, opening the back door. "My bag is in here somewhere. We just used them last night. Where'd I put those Trojans?" She kneeled on the seat, bending over to check the floor for her handbag.

"Maybe it's in the back," he said.

"The trunk?" she said. "Oh, maybe. Go pop it for me, okay?"

He wanted to pop more than the trunk, but he went around to the driver's side, opened the door and found what he hoped was the lever for the trunk.

It popped open slightly.

"I'll look," he said. He shut the door and went around to the back of the car and lifted the trunk.

The light hadn't come on in the trunk, so he rooted around in things, and threw a couple of suitcases out on the dirt. He reached into a pile of clothes, but they felt funny. He wondered why they felt so ragged.

Then he felt the top of Scratch's head.

3

He nearly jumped when he felt it. It was bumpy, but he knew he was touching bone. He laughed to himself at the slight chill he got from the contact. It was kind of gross having a dead little guy in the back, even if it was about five hundred years old.

He thought he found Tammy's little round suitcase, and as he reached for it, something grabbed him by the wrist.

It wasn't just a grab. It felt like razors on his skin.

For just a moment he thought he'd stuck his hand into one of the other guys' shaving kits, and somehow, someway their razor blades were all laying in a circle, like a bracelet on his wrist.

Then he felt a pain that shot from his hand up his elbow and finally ended at his jaw.

Something had scraped skin off his wrist.

He tried to bring his hand out, but whatever had it gripped it tight. It was like a bear trap on his wrist. His mind wasn't working right as he tried to see in the dark, among the piles of crap. The razors dug deeper and he screeched.

Maybe if he'd been over at the fire, like Josh and Bronwyn and Ziggy, they'd hear that as a metallic sound.

Maybe.

4

Tammy scrambled out of the car seat, and ran back to the trunk. She could make out Griff, but wasn't sure what she was really seeing. It looked like he was doing some kind of crazy fast dance. His arms were jerking around and his legs were all wobbly.

And then he began moving toward her, now slower, almost slow motion, and she saw something that looked almost like a small dog snapping at his heels.

"Griff?" she asked.

As he got closer to her, he whispered, "Help me. Help me. Get it off me."

She saw it, finally, as it scrambled up his back and perched on his shoulder, its teeth going into his neck.

She tried to scream, but her voice was gone. All she could do was whimper. She stood there, naked, watching Griff fall to the ground, to his knees, while something on top of him made the most awful sucking sound. A spray of blood hit Tammy across her face, across her breasts, and she tasted Griff's blood on her tongue.

And then her voice came back to her, and she screamed loud and long.

5

Before the three around the fire could register the scream, let alone get up and go running to them, Tammy remembered the gun. She tried to swallow the feeling of horror and shock inside her—*if you stop it gets you, move, girl, move and do something, don't just be scared, take action*—and she remembered Griff's gun. He kept it in his duffel bag. The duffel bag was in the trunk. If she could run around the other side of the car, she could get it. She knew she could. She had no other weapon. There was nothing else. Quickly, she turned around and ran. She heard a strange yelp from Griff's throat, which would be the last thing she'd ever hear from him.

Her mind spun a mile a minute as she tried to process what she had seen, what was happening, but her thoughts moved into a darker place where survival was more important than logic, and where nightmares could be faced. She reached into the trunk, and felt around the suitcases and the clothes, and then she found it. His duffel bag. She reached in, pulling out his dirty laundry. Her hand touched metal. The gun. She grabbed it. She wasn't even sure how to work it, but she knew it wasn't rocket science. Point, aim, pull trigger, fire.

She brought the gun up in the dark at the thing. Her hands were shivering so she kept both of them on the gun, holding it as steady as she could. She felt for the trigger. She tried to aim as best she could.

Griff fell completely to the earth, and that little thing was moving over him rapidly, its arms going up and then down on his body, and she saw what might have been scraps of . . . skin? It was skinning him?

Oh my god oh my god oh my god, she thought as she closed her eyes and squeezed the trigger. But she hadn't squeezed hard enough. *Come on. It's a gun. You can do it. You've watched TV. You know how guns are shot.* She squeezed it again, this time using all her strength.

She heard an explosion that was momentarily deafening, and saw a bright light. For the barest second, she saw it—the bloody mass that was Griff, and that Scratch thing, its claws going up and down like a Benihana chef as it skinned Griff. Blood poured everywhere.

She hadn't hit it. She hadn't hit anything. She hadn't even aimed well.

Scratch made gurgling sounds as it moved rapidly around Griff's body.

When a flashlight's beam hit its face—those turquoise eyes shiny green and alive in the light—it made a noise that was part growl and part shriek, grabbed something, and ran off into the darkness.

6

Josh stood there, his flashlight focused on Griff's body.

Bronwyn came up behind him, holding a long stick that burned at one end, like it was a torch.

Josh put the light on Tammy. She pointed the gun at him. "Tammy," Josh said.

The gun went off.

Josh instinctively fell to the ground.

"Tammy!" Bronwyn shouted. "Put the gun down now!"

Josh hit Tammy with the flashlight beam. Tammy's naked body was covered with blood. Her eyes seemed wide and vacant as she stared at them. Then she started screaming and wouldn't stop for the longest time.

7

Ziggy was shivering as if he'd been doused with ice-cold water. He kept the blanket wrapped tightly around him, and he was standing as close to the fire as he could get without burning himself. He kept turning slowly around and around as if sure that someone or something would pounce at any second. He rolled the fattest doobie he could, lit it up, and sucked in as much of the smoke as possible. The world turned into the blue haze of smoke with tongues of flames shooting up from the fire.

He saw something coming toward him in the dark—a low, thick shadow moving among the low scrub brush.

"Heya, Zigster," it was Griff's voice, and as the thing moved into the aura of light from the fire, he saw the little bastard monster with bloody skin all over him, moving rapidly forward, claws clicking, waving the skin of Griff's arms and hands like too-long sleeves from its own arms, and on its large skull head, Griff's face-skin, with eyeholes that showed shimmering green.

Ziggy felt his heart in his throat, and his pulse grew rapid. He took another toke and tried to get his feet to move, but something in the purple weed smoke seemed to make him feel safe. He was transfixed as the little bastard wearing Griff's skin moved around the fire, and came toward him.

"You ain't gonna get me," Ziggy said. "I'm high. I'm floatin'."

The little bastard scurried well around the fire, and Ziggy knew that it was the fire itself that scared the creep. Ziggy reached in and picked up the end of a stick from the edge of the fire. He waved the burning stick in front of him, slashing at the air.

He saw the green eyes through the bloody

skin. They seemed to be twitching. It was like the little bastard was thinking.

Ziggy took a step backward. He could run. He could climb into the fire and burn up to protect himself from the little bastard, or he could run.

He stood a chance if he ran.

"What are you thinking, you dumb stoner?" Griff's voice came from the creature. "You can run from the Great and Omnipotent Flayer of Men? You can't. This thing can run, boy, let me tell you. It can run like a jaguar. It can leap real high. It can do all kinds of things. But Zig, it ain't so bad. It really ain't. Getting your skin all torn off ain't the worst thing. It feels pretty good. It's sweet. It's about giving your life to something bigger than you. Something eternal."

Ziggy held his breath, and tried to get as stoned as he could off his last hit of weed.

And then, the little bastard leapt through the air, discarding Griff's skin, which floated slowly down into the fire as the creature latched on to Ziggy's balls.

8

"What in the world is that . . . stench?" Bronwyn asked. It was in the air—smoke from the fire off the road smelled like a barbeque gone bad. She and Josh and Tammy had been standing around the car, stunned. She had her arm over Tammy's shoulder. Tammy had finally calmed for a few seconds—enough time to lower the gun and quit shooting haphazardly.

Then they heard Ziggy's choking scream.

"Zig!" Tammy shouted.

She ran down the road, her arms raised up, gun in hand, no doubt terrified for her life.

Bronwyn began swearing, and Josh held his breath.

They both stood there one more second, and then Josh exhaled and said, "Ziggy."

9

Josh went running out on the desert, toward the fire. He felt he was moving too slow, and he saw Ziggy's red-lit face as he approached the fire, but it wasn't just the firelight—blood spurted up from his body. Josh got there just in time to watch the creature tear open Ziggy from neck to bowels. His steamy entrails poured out in loops. Ziggy's eyes seemed to follow his body being ripped open, and Josh wondered for a second if he could see it.

Josh stopped at the opposite side of the fire. He grabbed a stick from the flames. It was so hot that his hands felt as if they were burning, but he slashed it in the air, its trail of flame lighting up the night. As he got closer to the creature—now scraping at Ziggy's skin and laughing gleefully in a voice that was too close to Griff's—Josh began slamming the burning stick down on it. It squealed, and leapt up onto Ziggy's head, leaning over to scratch Ziggy's eyes out and hold them at the end of its black talons.

It stared at Josh, but it was nearly comical-looking. Its turquoise eyes seemed to change from blue to green and back to blue again. Now it spoke first with Griff's voice and then with Ziggy's, alternating back and forth as if, in tearing out both their throats, it had stolen their voices.

"Get away!" it screamed. "You son-of-a-bitch, this is your old pal! Come on, boy, get the hell away!"

As Josh brought the stick down to hit the creature's head, it leapt up as if it could fly, its claws spread wide, its arms impossibly long, and ran off into the night, letting out a shrill scream that sounded like the way Ziggy had screamed one night in his sleep.

Chapter Eleven

1

"Oh my God! Oh my God!" Tammy shouted while Bronwyn took a blanket and covered her. They had made it back to the fire without getting attacked. Josh stood on the other side, crouching over Ziggy's body.

Tammy's teeth were chattering so loudly that it was like some old typewriter noise, and she shivered as if she were freezing.

Josh stared at Bronwyn, who stared back at him. All three of them had tears streaming down their faces.

After several minutes, Josh said, "It's scared of fire."

Bronwyn, one arm still slung across Tammy's back, reached into her breast pocket and pulled out her Merits. She slid a cigarette between her lips, dropped the pack back in her pocket, withdrew her Bic lighter, flicked it, lit the cigarette, took the first puff and said, "What *is* that thing?"

"It's the Unspeakable Mystery," Tammy whimpered. "We let it out. We stole it. We're all gonna die! And not just die, we're all gonna get torn up just like Griff. Torn to itty-bitty pieces."

She hadn't actually seen Ziggy's body yet. Josh had laid a blanket over it, barely aware that he could function at all. Tammy looked around the campfire. "Where's Ziggy?"

Bronwyn raised her eyebrows to Josh, who went to the cooler and brought out a can of Pearl Beer. He tossed it to Bronwyn. She missed it, but picked it up off the ground and dusted it off with her hand. She popped the top and passed it to Tammy. "Take a sip. Come on. Take a sip," she said.

Too eagerly, Tammy grabbed the beer and chugged it down. When she was done, she dropped the can by her feet. "It got Ziggy, too."

Josh nodded.

"What's the plan?" Bronwyn asked.

"I don't know."

"We've got to make a plan. We've got Scratch coming at us."

Tammy started giggling. She covered her mouth, but couldn't contain it.

"What's funny?" Bronwyn asked.

"It's not happening," Tammy said. "Don't you see? There's no way in hell this can happen. It's all a trick. Some kind of trick. Griff must be in on it."

Bronwyn petted the top of Tammy's head like she was a puppy. Bronwyn leaned into her, touching her scalp to Tammy's cheek. "We'll get through this. Don't worry. Somehow."

Tammy guffawed, pulling away from Bron. "There's no way this is real. It can't be. There's no such thing as that . . . thing."

Josh went around the fire and sat next to Bronwyn. "What if each of us grabs a log from the fire. We walk over to the car. If we set the car on fire. Maybe . . ."

Bronwyn said, "Maybe. Maybe not. Don't you have flares in the Pimpmobile?"

2

Josh brought his flashlight into the trunk of the car, and shone it around the clothes and luggage. He pulled some of the suitcases out, and the bags of clothes.

Then he reached down and drew something out.

Bronwyn and Tammy huddled together, each with a burning stick in her hand.

Josh held up a small cylindrical object. "One flare, coming up."

3

Back at the campfire, Josh had to wrangle with the flame a bit to get it to work. When he snapped it, it shot out into the air.

A brilliant, ragged orange-yellow streak of light. He set it down on the ground.

They all looked at it.

"No one's going to help us," Tammy said. "No one."

Bronwyn glanced at her watch. "It's almost midnight. Maybe six hours 'til daylight."

"What good's daylight," Tammy said. "We'll be dead by then."

"We could start walking along the road."

"Someone will see that flare," Josh said.

"No one is going to see that flare unless they're looking for us. That monster is going to come back," Tammy said. "It's going to cut us all up. It . . . it . . . it." She hiccupped this last part.

"We should go to the road. We should start walking," Bronwyn said. "We can keep lighting sticks, one after another and then drop them when they burn out. We have the flashlight."

"What if we walk the wrong way?" Josh asked.

"I'm not sure there is a wrong way."

"What if it's there, out there on the road?"

"I think it's gone," Bronwyn said. "Let's assume that it's the Flesh-Scraper. Let's assume it got enough flesh. Let's assume that's all it wanted."

Josh wanted to go to her and hold her—she looked haunted now. She looked as if she'd gone from being a young woman of twenty to being fifty. She looked as if she had enormous sorrow at the center of her being, and he wanted to make it better for her somehow.

Looking between Bronwyn and Tammy, he wasn't sure what the hell he could do. He wanted to cry out to his father and mother to come get him. He wanted to find someone to protect him, but when he looked at the two of them, some other instinct came out within him. He wasn't sure what to call it, other than something more than the will to survive. It was something that seemed to wrestle deep inside his mind, something that made him want to protect his two friends, although he wasn't sure that was possible. But another part of him just wanted to be safe himself, to get away from this place, to somehow wake up from this nightmare.

Tammy leaned forward and tapped Bronwyn to pass her another beer. "Please, I need it," she said. Bronwyn opened two, passed one to her, and began drinking one of the cans herself. Tammy chugged this one also, and let her blanket slip. Josh was so stunned by the night's events that he barely noticed Tammy's nakedness beneath the blanket.

Tammy wiped at the blood on her face as if it were water. "That thing talked. I heard it."

Josh nodded. "I did, too."

"This fries my brain," Bronwyn said, sipping the beer. "Am I the only one who feels as if everything I ever heard of in life was a lie?"

"Maybe this is what happens before you die," Tammy said. "I been bad in my life. Real bad. Maybe that's the devil. Maybe that thing is the devil. It sounded just like Griff. Poor Griff."

"It's the ritual," Josh said. "When Griff pushed me over and I fell on it, it got some of my blood and some of my skin. That's what the sign said. You turn it on that way. And now it's skinning them."

They all said nothing for several minutes, each one looking out into the darkness beyond the flickering fire.

"Where'd it get Ziggy?" Tammy asked.

Finally, Bronwyn broke the silence. "He's over there." She pointed to the blanket at the edge of where the firelight stretched, opposite them.

"We never knew his real name," Josh said. "Just Ziggy."

"James Wallace," Bronwyn said. "I heard it on the first day of one of our classes. That's his name."

"James Wallace," Josh said. "Rest in peace."

Tammy closed her eyes and began saying the Lord's Prayer aloud.

"Stop it," Bronwyn said.

Tammy opened her eyes and turned to her. "You got something better? I think we need to call on a higher power."

"If God gave a rat's ass about us," Bronwyn said, "He'd never have created that thing in the first place."

A strange and probably insane light seemed to brighten Tammy's eyes. "Maybe that's it. Maybe this is God's way of giving us purpose."

"Say what?"

"Maybe we're meant to undergo this. Like a trial. When I used to go to revivals, they talked about how God tested you. How the devil tempted . . . and you need to believe in Jesus's power. That's what we need."

"Well, I guess being the Jew here, I'm outta luck," Bronwyn said.

"No, just accept Jesus," Tammy said. She had a weird little smile that Bronwyn wanted to slap out of her. "If you accept Jesus in your heart, it'll be okay. We can get out of this. Through Jesus."

"Oh Christ," Bronwyn said. "Just keep drinking the Pearl Beer, Tammy."

"It takes on the voices of the ones it skins," Josh said.

4

Bronwyn said, "I say we start walking." She pushed herself up from the ground. "We have fire. We have what's left of that flashlight battery. If we walk fast, we can do more than three miles per hour. Tammy, you run cross-country."

She nodded.

"We could even try to run," Bronwyn said. "At least some of the way. Maybe Jesus will help you run."

"Do not tempt the savior," Tammy said.

"When did you get so religious?" Bronwyn asked.

"Since I saw that thing tear Griff open. Since all

123

this," Tammy said, still with that weird light on her face that made Josh and Bronwyn both think of the movie *Song of Bernadette*.

"Scratch moves pretty fast," Josh said, then noticed Bronwyn's arched eyebrows. "We're on a first-name basis."

"It might not even want us. But if we walk that-a-way," Bronwyn pointed to the road, "maybe we stand a chance."

"Not if it gets us," Tammy said, keeping her eyes on the fire.

"It might be full," Josh said, though he felt a little sick at the thought. "I mean, if I remember right, it said on those signs that it drank the blood and wore the skins and used the meat for food. I mean, when spiders eat one fly, they don't always eat more."

"Yeah, but they wrap them up for later," Bronwyn chortled, and then covered her mouth. "I can't believe I'm making a joke."

"You feel that, too? That light-headedness?" Josh whispered as if it were a dirty secret.

Bronwyn nodded. "Yup. It must be shock."

He got up and went to the outer ring of light and vomited. He came back, popped a beer open, and guzzled it. "I'm talking like a nutcase. Maybe it's shock. Maybe it's just insanity. Loony tunies. I got the loony tunies."

"We all have them," Bronwyn said. "What do we do? Sit here until it comes back?"

"The car," Josh said. "It's like a tank. We put a ring of fire around it, and we wait. That thing didn't break out through the trunk. It can't do that. We're safest in the car. Someone will have seen the flare, and will see the ring of fire around the car. And they'll come."

5

Someone had seen the flare out in the middle of that desert hellhole: Billy Dunne. He and Dave Olshaker, whose ass still stung from rock salt shot out of Charlie Goodrow's shotgun, were staying at a Motel 69 five miles out of a town called Naga. They were a good fifteen miles to the northeast, off the two-lane road that ventured off the highway that had ventured—via several other roads—off the main highway. Billy was just coming back from picking up some burgers and fries from a local drive-through, and as he drove down a desolate one-lane road back to the highway, he briefly saw in the distance a strange orange light. Back at Motel 69, he told Dave, who was in bed already watching *Mork & Mindy*. Dave went out to the parking lot, and Billy pointed to the general direction.

"It's gotta be them," Dave said, wolfing down his hamburger, with its sauce and mayo dribbling down his chin. "I know they're up there. We know they're outta gas. We gotta go find 'em, Billy."

"What do we do with them?" Billy asked.

Dave snarled, "First, we just grab Tammy and get the hell out of there."

"It was smart to siphon their tank," Billy said.

"It was a stroke of genius if I do say so myself," Dave Olshaker said.

6

Their evening had been none too pleasant. When they'd arrived at the Brakedown Palace, Dave had gone in after Tammy, and had left instructions for Billy to empty their gas tank so they couldn't take off too fast. The place had been empty, so he followed the long corridor out into the long Quonset hut, along the creepy trail to the final room where, suddenly, all hell was breaking loose. Charlie Goodrow had begun shooting at everybody, Dave included, and got him right in the left butt cheek with a powerful spray of rock salt. At first, he thought he'd been hit with a real bullet, but then, with the stinging, he knew exactly what it was.

While Tammy and her jerk friends took off in their car, he was stuck behind with Charlie Goodrow, who had threatened to call the police.

"Go ahead and call 'em," Dave had said. "They should be thrown in jail for everything they've done."

Charlie Goodrow had looked at him long and hard, and set down his shotgun. "You're not with them?"

"Not hardly," Dave said. He pointed to Billy Dunne. "Me and him's been tracking them, because the snake with the blond hair stole my girl right out from under me."

"They stole my attraction," Charlie Goodrow said. "But . . . well, I guess I shouldn't call the police just yet."

"Call 'em," Dave said. "Please. They deserve arresting."

But Charlie Goodrow, for some reason Dave couldn't figure out, wouldn't call the cops. He said something about things being better left alone sometimes. Something about worse things coming when good went after bad.

Instead, Goodrow told Dave and Billy to get the hell out of his gas station before he pulled the shotgun out again.

Then, Dave and Billy had decided they'd lost their classmates for good. They got the motel room and figured they'd better turn around that night. "You don't need her," Billy said, his arm over his buddy's shoulder. "You can do better than her."

"Yeah, she's a bitch," Dave said, shrugging off his friend's arm. He didn't feel comfortable like that. It felt wrong.

But now, looking out at the dark night, after midnight, the sting in his ass didn't feel quite so bad. He thought of what he'd do to her if he had her. If he got her. First he'd tie her wrists to the bed, then strip her, using his teeth to tear her clothes off. Then he'd give her what she wanted most from him. He got hard, standing there, thinking about it.

He said, "Billy, let's get on up to those hills up there. We gotta track 'em down."

7

Billy Dunne felt like he was driving in circles for nearly an hour before Dave looked ahead in the dark and pointed to something off another road to the west. "Look, that must be them," he said. Billy glanced over and saw what looked like a fire off the road. "This is too easy," Dave said. "They're stranded. They got nothin'. My dream's coming true, Billy. Truer than true."

Billy swerved and made a U-turn and then went west on a slender, barely paved road and then went north. He nearly hit a coyote as he drove, and he thought for just a second that he felt Dave's hand on his knee.

8

Josh had just finished positioning some rocks and dry sticks about ten feet away from the Pimpmobile. Then he helped Tammy arrange some on the other side. She'd dressed again, at first scared to reach into the trunk, but he'd used the flashlight to show her that no monsters lurked there. Then they'd set to work, and in some respects, setting up the circle of fire as a perimeter around the Pimpmobile took all their minds off the terror that was somewhere out in the desert.

"Maybe it's over," Tammy said. She sat on the

hood of the car, cross-legged. The fires comforted her.

"Could be," Josh said.

"Someone has to feed the fire," Bronwyn said.

"We'll take turns." Then he noticed the doubtful look on Bronwyn's face. "Someone will see this. There's a town within twenty miles of here. The flare went up. Now we have a large fire."

"They may just think it's a fire. Nobody lives up here. Nobody cares if there's a fire," Bronwyn said. "There's not enough to burn."

"That's not true," Josh said. "Fires on the desert can get out of control. It can be devastating if it spreads. Someone will see this from a distance. I bet you can see it for miles."

"We can't see a town. I'm not sure they can see us."

"Someone's driving out there. Someone's on the roads. They'll see it and stop somewhere and maybe call the police," he said. "You have to believe."

"I believe," Tammy said. "I believe that Jesus Christ is my personal savior and is the son of the everlasting God."

"Good for you," Josh said.

"I'll pray for all of us," Tammy said.

When Josh went around to make sure there was some dry brush to toss in one of the fires, Bronwyn followed him. "I didn't want to say this in front of her."

"What's that?"

"Josh. How can this be happening? Can you tell me?" She seemed like a little girl, even with the cigarette hanging out of her mouth. "How is this humanly possible?"

"I guess it's not," he said.

She smoked some more, and he almost thought he saw tears streaming down her face. "Can you hold me?" she asked. "Right now. I know it's . . ." She was about to say "weird," he was certain, but he didn't let her get to that word. He went over to her and put his arms around her. She laid her head against his shoulder and began sobbing. "We'll get through this," he whispered, smelling her hair and feeling weak and strong at the same time.

9

Tammy was the first to get sleepy, and Josh promised her that he'd stand guard. He told Bronwyn to go sleep for a bit, also. "We have the fire, and we know it doesn't like fire. It's not going to cross over to the car. But if it did, you're inside a metal cage in that car. I doubt even obsidian claws can get through a car door," he said.

"Only if you sit in the car, too," she said. "I want you safe."

Tammy and Bronwyn lay together across the backseat, using blankets and rolled-up clothes as pillows. Josh sat up front, his one hand on the gun, his other on the Bic lighter as if this would help ward off Scratch. He kept looking around, feeling like he heard things. He didn't know what good it would do, but he locked the doors. He felt sleepy, but fought it. All the beer had done a number on him, and he felt exhausted and drained on top of that—but he didn't want to sleep. Not that night. He was going to stay awake. He could sleep all day long if he had to, once they got to safety.

Suddenly, without even thinking he'd closed his eyes, he was on a waterbed that undulated with gentle waves. Bronwyn and Tammy were there, too. They were both naked, kissing each other sweetly, nothing too dirty, and playing innocently with each other's breasts. Tammy reached over and grabbed his hand and brought it down between her legs. Then they were not naked at all, nor were they the two women from his college. Instead, he was back home, and it was his mother and his aunt who grabbed his hands and were taking him to school. His aunt said, "You never told us that you didn't pass your chemistry final."

"But I did," he said, or tried to, but no one seemed to hear him. His mother gave him a stern look, and she let go of his hand. Suddenly he was back in high school, but it wasn't full of high school students—instead, the children looked as if they were nine or ten. He was in elementary school—he was sure of it. How had this happened? He tried to tell the teacher who came to get him that he was already in college, that he shouldn't have to go back to the fifth grade, but the teacher—Mrs. Raleigh, who had once humiliated him in front of the entire fifth grade—told him that he needed to mind his P's and Q's. "But this isn't right!" he shouted. "I'm almost twenty." The other kids in the fifth grade looked at him funny, but paid very little attention to him. He noticed something even worse: He had no pants on. He sat there in his shirt, but no pants, no underwear. Hanging out. And no one said anything. Why hadn't his mother noticed? How could she have let him leave the house without his pants on? He tried to pull his shirt down over his balls, but it wouldn't go far enough.

And then someone began banging at the window of the classroom. Someone was yelling at him.

Josh opened his eyes, wrenched from the dream.

10

Tammy had already begun screaming—not just screaming, but it was like the sound cats made when they were in heat, a wail that barely sounded human. Bronwyn was up, and apparently had been shaking Josh.

"It's gonna get us!" Tammy screamed. "Oh my God, it's gonna kill us!"

But Josh saw headlights out the window. And then, like a nightmare come true, Dave Olshaker's face suddenly appeared against the windshield. "Hey, you losers! How's it hangin'?"

11

"Get out of here!" Bronwyn shouted.

"How the hell did they get here?" Josh said, still wondering whether this might be an extension of his dream.

Bronwyn had to slap Tammy to get her to stop screaming. Dave and his buddy were shaking the car up and down, trying the doors, running around the car.

"We should tell them," Bronwyn said.

"Are you crazy? Keep your doors locked. That guy's insane," Josh said. He had already dropped the gun on the floor of the Pimpmobile.

Dave was shouting, "Tammy! You're coming with me, baby! Do you understand?"

"Don't let him take me," Tammy said.

"They have a car," Josh said. "Oh my God. We can get out."

Bronwyn rolled her window down slightly. "Hey! Guys! We know you're mad. We know it. But there's some kind of . . ." She paused, unsure of what to say. "There's a killer out here. We need help."

"Griff is dead!" Tammy shouted. "Griff is dead!"

It probably was this cry that stopped Dave Olshaker in his tracks. He and Billy Dunne looked at each other for a second. Dave started laughing.

"Oh my God," Bronwyn said. Josh looked back at her. She was looking toward the headlights of

133

the pickup truck. "They ruined part of our fire. Part of the ring we made."

"So?" He turned and saw the break in the circle of fire.

"What if it's been out there? Waiting? Just outside the fire?"

"No, it's not," Josh said.

But just as quickly, they all heard a woman's high-pitched scream. Josh looked at Tammy but her mouth was closed.

It was Billy Dunne.

Or rather, it wasn't Billy Dunne.

He had been there, standing just in the headlights in front of the Pimpmobile, and suddenly, he was gone.

They heard a thud beneath the car.

Dave Olshaker glanced around the car, stepping back from it.

Inside the car, they were silent.

Josh said, *"Just go away. Just go."*

"Billy?" Dave walked around the car. "Billy?"

"We've got to let him in," Josh said, leaning over to unlock the driver's side door.

"No," Tammy said. "Don't let him in." She had a curious anger in her voice.

"Dave!" Josh shouted. "Dave, come around here, get in!"

But Dave Olshaker was looking around the car, crouching down as if looking under it.

"Don't let him in," Tammy said.

"Tammy?" Bronwyn asked, softly.

"He did something bad to me," she said. "Maybe this is what happens to bad people. Maybe . . ."

"Dave!" Josh said, rolling his window all the way down, signaling for Olshaker to get over there. He was about to open his door to pull Dave in, when suddenly they all heard it.

The voice from under the car.

"Davy baby," Billy Dunne's voice rasped. "Sweetie, come to Daddy. You know you love me, Davy, all hidden away inside you. I love you, too, we can love each other here, down here."

"What in God's name?" Dave said, still crouching.

"Don't let him in, Josh," Tammy spat. "Let it happen to him. Let it. Maybe bad people get what's coming to them."

"Shut up," Bronwyn said. "Just shut up."

"Dave! Get in this car right now! There's some kind of . . . some . . . that thing. That thing from the gas station. It's there. It's alive. It's . . ." But even as Josh said this, he knew it was too late.

He looked out his window to see Dave, still crouching, glance up at him, his eyes wide with an emotion between fear and awe. Dave began stammering, and pointing underneath the car. It seemed to happen in slow motion, as Dave pointed and looked at Josh and his mouth began moving as if trying to get something out.

And then Scratch leapt out from beneath the car, its black hooks going to Dave's eyes. In the car, everyone was screaming, and Josh reached on the floor for the gun hoping it would help. He tried to get his door open, but it was locked. By the time he reached around for the lock, Dave's face had smushed up against Bronwyn's window. The two women screamed again as Dave's bloody face slid down the window to the ground.

Josh locked his door, rolled up his window.

And they waited. It was quiet for a long time.

The headlights from the pickup truck illuminated them as if it were nearly daylight.

They heard a thump or two beneath the car.

Tammy began praying softly, her hands pressed together, her eyes closed. Josh glanced at Bronwyn, but neither said anything.

They saw something come out from under the front of the car that sent shivers down Josh's spine.

The creature emerged in the headlight's beam. Billy Dunne's face over its skull, his lips torn and flapping. It began a strange, slow dance that reminded Josh of an image he'd seen of Kali, the Indian goddess, who danced with skulls around her neck. The creature's arms went out at odd angles, and its legs moved around in wide arcs.

It's doing its dance, Josh thought. *This is its ceremony. It drinks the blood and wears the skin. It dances in the skin. It makes the sacrifice dance for the gods.*

Josh felt Bronwyn's hand on his shoulder. It felt good, in the face of this. He needed her warmth.

They watched the strange, intricate, bizarre

dance as the bloodied creature wearing the tissue-thin skin of either Billy Dunne or Dave Olshaker moved to the unheard music.

Then it stopped.

It's watching us. It's waiting for us. Why? What is it waiting for?

A sound came from it. Not Dave's voice or Billy's voice or Griff's or even Ziggy's.

It was a sound that seemed more wild animal than human, yet it had a human cast to it. The creature began singing, raising its skin-hung arms skyward.

"Dear God," Tammy gasped. "Dear God."

The creature sang a tuneless melody that consisted of mainly open vowel sounds of *ohs* and *ows*, a slightly musical howl and shriek, but Josh was sure it was saying something.

"Why is it doing that?" Bronwyn asked—as if any of them would know.

"It has a ceremony to fulfill," Josh said. "A ritual. It dances in their skins, and then it sings to its namesake god. That's what it said at the Brakedown Palace. On the signs. There's the sacrifice, then there's the ceremony."

Even as he said this, Josh thought he heard the god's name in the song, *Xipe Totec, Xipe Totec*.

What is it for? Why does it do this? For the first time, Josh wondered whether there wasn't some insane logic to the creature's ritual. It wasn't just a monster from nowhere. It had been stolen from its resting place, somewhere in Mexico. It had been wrenched from its burial ground and brought up here by some moron who decided to make a buck off it—or seventy-five cents—and forget that it was sacred.

He said it aloud: "Scratch is sacred."

"What?" Bronwyn asked, as if Josh were losing more marbles than he had moments before.

"That thing is a representation of a god. Xipe Totec. The Flayer of Men. We're seeing an ancient ceremony."

"Christ, you're starting to make sense."

"I don't know what good it does us unless you can remember what was on those signs. What else was written there," Josh said.

"We can make it to the pickup truck," Tammy said. "If we run. We can."

"No," Josh said. "We can't. It's too far. That thing is right there, Tammy."

"If all three of us go," Tammy said. "It'll only get one of us."

"Who will it be? You? Me? Bron? You can live with that?"

"Either that or we all die sitting here."

"We're safe here," Josh said. He reached back over his seat and touched her gently on the knee. "Tammy, just hang in there. I don't think it can get in the car. It may need night for its ritual. It may not be after us during the day."

"Or maybe it just doesn't stop," Tammy said. "What about that? Maybe it'll be morning soon and that thing will still be waiting to get us. Or maybe it'll figure out how to scratch its way through the car. Maybe."

"Tammy, listen to Josh," Bronwyn said. "We've all been through a big shock. But it hasn't gotten to us here."

"The battery in that truck is going to die. Sometime in the next hour or two," Tammy said. "If we don't get out and make a run for it, we may never get out of here. We are already dead, if you think about it. We just haven't had our moment with that monster."

The singing in front of the car continued, and the creature they had all begun to think of as Scratch waved its claws to the sky as if talking directly to its god.

12

Perhaps an hour went by before the headlights of Dave Olshaker's truck flickered a bit. Then they dimmed. Scratch had gone off into the darkness somewhere, and Josh guessed that it was either under the pickup or under the Pimpmobile.

"We can sit here and die, or . . ." Tammy said, after they'd all been too quiet and too tense and too watchful for too long. It was a surprise to hear her voice.

More of a surprise, she opened her door, and jumped out in the dirt, slamming the door behind her.

Before they could say anything, she was running

in the dimming headlights for the pickup truck. Josh held his breath, watching her, but he was sure he saw her open the driver's door and slam it again. He heard her shouts of joy. "I'm inside! I'm inside!"

And then, she flicked on the truck's interior light to see the layout of keys and pedals.

And Bronwyn said what Josh was thinking. "I can't look. I can't look. I can't." She repeated it over and over again, even while they both stared out at Tammy and her completely heroic and insane act to try and get out of this hellhole.

The truck was moving forward, toward them, and Tammy had a big grin on her face like all her prayers had been answered.

But Bronwyn and Josh both saw some little movement in the back of the cab of the truck.

It was in there, with her.

Josh opened his door, with Bronwyn shouting at him. He ran toward the truck. By the time he reached Tammy's side, Scratch had already began throwing her around, and when Josh opened the door, it had dragged her out the opposite window, trailing blood.

The whole time, Tammy hadn't screamed. He was sure that the last look on her face had been, not one of terror, but of submission.

She hadn't even fought.

Perhaps she couldn't have fought.

He'd never know.

Twenty minutes later, out in the darkness, they heard Tammy's last shrill scream, although they couldn't be sure whether it was actually Tammy or Scratch imitating her voice.

Josh ran back to the Pimpmobile and had to pull Bronwyn out of the backseat. "We can get out, let's go," he said. They ran back to the truck and climbed in. Josh put the truck in first gear, and it moved forward.

"It's over," Bronwyn said. "We can go. We can help. Oh thank God. Thank you, God. Thank you."

They got just about a mile past the ring of fire they'd created, and the pickup truck died.

"It's the battery," Josh said.

The headlights dimmed to nothingness. They rolled up both windows, locked the doors, and checked to make sure everything in the cab was secure.

Exhausted, they folded into one another. Josh managed to close his eyes for a few minutes and not think of the horror.

Now and then, he awoke, because Scratch's claws raked around the side of the pickup truck. They had no light. He'd left the gun and flashlight back in the Pimpmobile. Maybe the Bic lighter was something, but he didn't want to waste it.

It was only two hours until dawn. He and Bronwyn sat up, and kept watch, but Bronwyn told him it might be better if they slept. "Maybe in our sleep, when it kills us, it won't be so bad."

Chapter Twelve

1

"What if this is it?" Bronwyn asked. It was still dark—an endless night.

"It what?"

"It. Our last night on this earth. What if we don't get out? What if that thing kills us both?"

"You can't believe that. You can't. There's a way."

"I wonder if Griff thought that. Or Tammy. Or Ziggy." She lit what must've been her twentieth cigarette of the night. "It's like we're drowning in the ocean and there's a great white shark coming at us. Instead of water, all this dirt. What if this is it?"

She lowered the cigarette and leaned into him. Kissed him. Her lips were soft, dry, and yet somehow he felt moistened by them. She looked at him steadily. She no longer looked like a college girl. She no longer looked like a girl he was interested in. She looked like a woman who was preparing for something. And he knew what it was. Not death. But sex. Warmth. Lust.

Something human and animal, hot and cold at the same time, something nearly predatory, seemed to take over within him. He kissed her again, tasting the ashes of her smoky breath, and then he reached around and held her, pressing himself close. She moved gently against him.

If his mind warned him against this, his body didn't listen. They wrapped around each other, and she pushed him backward. She was all over him, and he scrambled against her. Soon they were thrusting and licking, as uncomfortable as the truck was. He felt as if it were like his dream: The two of them in a great green forest. The *God, I love yous* were whispered, the hungry gasps and the slushy sounds of the two of them pressing and releasing, kissing and lapping at each other. He entered her body, felt an intense warm embrace, and it shot the feeling up his spine right into his skull—a ripple of lightning—as she tossed and twisted her body to accommodate him and enjoy the breadth of his flesh. He kissed her neck as she twisted around so that he was now behind her, grasping her breasts in his hand, his lower body thrusting faster and faster. She was moaning and whispering, "Yeah, oh, yeah, oh, oh." A slamming wave of thrusts ended as he reached his climax, as she reached hers, as they fell on top of each other—sweaty, burning, drained, full.

Afterward, he remembered too much, and drew

back from her. Had it been a dream, after all? Had he dreamt that he'd made love to her? He wasn't sure. Is that what people did when monsters were after them? Take a break to mate? Bond sexually so they could face death more easily? He felt older than he wanted to feel. He felt as if he'd crossed some great chasm in life—and looking back at his life before that night, it had all seemed pampered and silly and wasteful. Life and death were too important to play around with now. Even college seemed ridiculous—another ceremonial dance like the one Scratch had done for them. It was not about life and the struggle to survive one single night when faced with danger. He went to pull his clothes back on, and she came up behind him, kissing him on the neck. "I'm glad we did that," she said.

"Me three," he joked.

"You love me, don't you?"

He didn't respond. Then he thought better of it. "I don't know. Maybe."

"I'm sorry. It's not good to be in love at a time like this." She laughed. "Oh my God, the sun!"

And it was true. To the east, a lighter purple came up, bringing with it a misty halo around the mesas and mountains.

"I don't want to die!" she shouted to the still-lingering dark blue sky.

"Me neither!" he shouted.

"I want to live, damn it!"

"Me too!"

"I want to get middle-aged and fat and watch

bad TV and raise four kids into neurotic adults. I want to see China and learn how to water ski!"

"I want to grow old and die in a nursing home!" he shouted. "No, I want to die when I step off the curb in a big city, and a crazy taxi driver comes out of nowhere and hits me so that I bounce off the rest of the cars going too fast through the yellow light!"

"I want to die with my head in a bowl of green pea puree, with my Depends on, with only three teeth in my mouth!" she shouted, laughing.

Then they got quiet again.

He closed his eyes, and said a prayer.

"Know what?"

"What's that?"

"This is a bad dream," she said. "I bet that's all it is. I bet I'm sleeping on the lawn with you. Hung over. I bet it's the Saturday we left campus. The bitch of it is trying to wake up."

The day had officially begun, with the sun stretching molten gold an hour later. Heat came up too suddenly.

Bronwyn took a drag off the cigarette. Rolled down the window.

"Bron, it may still be out there," he said.

"It's a creature of the night, that's what the sign said. 'The Sun God is its enemy.'" She grinned, and then looked a little grim. He practically could read her mind: It was ridiculous to feel happy after the carnage of last night. But they did. Both of them did. They'd survived the night. She held her cigarette up in the morning air. She leaned back, and looked up at the vague sun, melted as it was into a pure yellow sky.

"If it's still out here, maybe it's sleeping," Josh said.

"It doesn't sleep," she said. She puffed out dragon breath. Sucked on the cigarette until it nearly disappeared between her lips. "I wonder what it's all about?"

"The creature?"

"No," she said, her voice carrying the quality of Ziggy's when he was at his most stoned. She was ragged, and when he looked at her, he thought she was beautiful despite the half-circles under her eyes and the skin drawn tight around her lips. "No, you know how life is this thing? This thing that you grow up doing because you think one day . . . one day you'll get to this . . . I don't know . . ."

"Wisdom?"

"Yeah. Wisdom. Knowledge. You've known something because there's this key you turn, and you don't get the key or even know which door to go to when you're a kid. You assume grown-ups have it. You assume education brings it to you. Or experience. And then, here we are. You believe in God, don't you?"

"Sometimes."

"I don't. Not at all. I used to think all religion was just a big lie. But after last night, I started thinking that maybe people came up with God and religion to give hope. Maybe hope isn't a real thing, but people need it because otherwise life is just this jungle where you wait to see what ends up jumping out of nowhere and eating you. And you have God. You have order. You have a reason. You have hope."

"Sometimes when I'm not sure I believe in God, I think of goodness."

She glanced over at him.

"That's all God is. Goodness. That there's goodness here. On earth. That it's our job to find it. To create it. To keep it going. Like a flame in your hand. Like a little fire everyone can hold if they want to. And it means fighting sometimes. It means standing up to darkness."

Bronwyn sat up, leaning forward. "On that note, I have to go take a leak," she said. She opened the door, and slid down out of the truck. He gasped for a second, his heart seeming to leap out of his chest. But nothing happened. No Scratch showed up suddenly, its claws extended.

She squatted down beside the truck. "Don't see any monsters under here," she said. He looked the other way to give her a little privacy. He had to go pee, too, so he got out and went around, peeing on a sagebrush.

They found a cooler with Coke and even some Twinkies in the back of the truck. They devoured these like it was the finest meal in existence.

Then they saw the siphon and the red plastic gas tank sitting at one end of the truck.

"Wow," he said.

"Wow is right," she added. "I guess we have Dave to thank for this."

"We're all to blame," he said. "All of us."

2

"We're probably going to die," she said, mid-Twinkie.

"Everybody dies."

They had begun walking back to the Pimpmobile to put what Josh had called "Plan B" into effect. He lugged the full plastic gas container, and she held the siphon and an extra Twinkie.

"Is that okay by you?" she asked.

"No. It's not okay. Today is not our day to die. That's all I know," Josh said. "This is not the day."

"They're all dead. All of them," she said.

"Maybe last night was their night. Maybe it was," Josh said. He swallowed a little dust, but felt better. Felt fear leaving his body as if through sheer force of will. "I'm not going to give in to this. We are alive now. We have some water. It can't be more than twenty miles out to the highway. Twenty miles is doable. Two gallons of gas will get us there."

"It's going to be hot as hell in an hour. Or less."

"So we'll get sunburnt."

"And it's going to find us."

"We don't know that. Are you just going to wait around, Bronwyn? Are you going to just sit there and let that thing tear you up like you were bait for a mountain lion? Think of it as a mountain lion. Don't get psyched by its claws. Or how we saw it at that gas station. We haven't seen it fly. It hasn't grown nine feet tall. It's little. Sure, it's fast. It's smart, maybe. Maybe not. But whatever you and I have, whatever is buried inside us that's going to come out someday . . . someday, years from now . . . I mean, what if you are destined to be a hero of life? What if I am? What if you go on to medical school and get into research and become the first doctor to cure cancer? What if I go on to write the book that changes lives? Is it worth us giving up now to this stupid little nasty monstrous . . . little bastard? Are we going to let it win just because we're afraid? Are we?"

Bronwyn gasped. "I've never seen you like this."

He sighed, but felt a steely resolve take him over. "I've never had to be like this."

Everything hurt inside him, every bit of him felt raw and raked, but he locked into the mindset that he knew he had to have.

The Pimpmobile came into view.

Bronwyn dropped the siphon when she saw what had happened to it.

3

Scratch had been busy in the night. The Pimpmobile's doors were off their hinges. The trunk was open, and all the crap from it was spread out on the ground.

Worse, as they got closer, the interior was ripped to shreds, and wires had been pulled and cut.

And the keys were gone.

"You know," Bronwyn said. "I think we better start walking while we still have Twinkies in us."

Josh set down the gas, sat on the shredded backseat, and began weeping like a baby.

Bronwyn put her arms around him and whispered, "Come on. Let's go. We'll get away from it. We have the whole day."

4

"Okay, what do we know about it?"

They walked side by side, Bronwyn with a slight limp, but she leaned on him now and then. They both guesstimated a general south-westerly direction to the main highway, although all they could see for miles was just more desert and mesas and arroyos and caverns and mountains in nearly every direction. They stuck to the road.

"You studied the Aztecs, didn't you?"

"I read a book. I didn't exactly study them. I just don't remember the details," she said.

"Remember. Force yourself to remember. You have to."

She stopped, closed her eyes.

"I can't."

"You can. What was on the cover?"

"An Aztec calendar."

151

"Good. So it was round and stone and had a face on it."

"Something like that."

"First page?"

"I don't think that thing is really from the ancient Aztecs," she said. "It's something else. They just made up all the stuff."

"Well, we know it hates the sun. And it loves the dark. And it skins people. And drinks blood."

"Oh I know," she said, "it's a vampire."

"I only wish," he said.

They continued walking, and he pointed out a snake moving along the edge of the road, so they stepped to the side, but kept walking.

"All right. It had a job. It skinned those who had been sacrificed. What about the ritual?"

"I just don't know."

"Try."

After another ten minutes, she said, "All right. Okay. It was an obsidian dagger. Used for the sacrificial victims. Tore their hearts out. The blood was like rain. They let the blood rain down because it was to encourage rain and the crops. The Flesh-Scraper was used to get the skin off."

"To wear it," Josh said, solemnly.

"Right."

"And somehow, it fed off Griff first. Was it blood?"

"I think so. I don't know."

"It'd make sense if it was blood."

"Wait," Bronwyn said. "Wait."

She stopped.

"Rain," she said. "Rain. Water. Liquid. It needs it. It's not just taking their skin. It drank them. It drained them. It needs water—water in the blood. It's a desert here. It needs water. It brings rain. That's its ritual."

"That was a rain dance? Last night?"

"Maybe," she said. "The enemy is the Sun God."

5

"This road is endless," she said.

"Thank God," he said.

"Have we been walking for hours?"

"Feels like it."

"You thirsty?"

"Mean thirsty."

"We must've gone twenty miles by now," she said.

"At least."

"Wrong direction," she said, too sadly. She pointed ahead.

He looked up—he'd been mainly watching the road for snakes and lizards.

The road just ended.

It ended into a dusty nothingness.

"We're not very bright," Josh said. He was soaked with sweat, exhausted, and had begun to wish that he'd just stayed back at Dave Olshaker's pickup truck.

"Wait," she said. "Wait! Oh my God! Oh my God!" Bronwyn began jumping up and down. "Where the road ends! Oh my God, Josh! Josh!" She was so gleeful he had thought she'd gone insane for good.

She began running to the west, across what looked like a well-beaten dirt path.

He looked in the direction where she'd run. Something shiny over the rise of land.

She stopped, turning around. She cupped her hands to her mouth and shouted, "Ely! He told us! He said he lives where the road ends! Do you hear it? I can. I can hear his ZZ Top records! He's playing them! Oh my God, Josh, we're safe! We're safe!"

Her enthusiasm lasted three more miles. The closer they got, the more they saw the hubcaps outside what looked like a large shack with a trailer behind it. ZZ Top's "Tush" played from within the house. They went to the front door and rapped at it.

After a while, the truck driver they'd met briefly, who had given them a lift to the Brakedown Palace, opened the door.

6

An hour later, something that the entire town of Naga believed was a miracle occurred. It began raining. At first, it was a small trickle of rain, and then clouds swiftly overtook the fire of the sun. Thunder was heard in the mesas, and a bitter storm swept the desert.

Josh slept, his arms around Bronwyn. When night came, he went out into the rain with Ely, who asked him what had happened to his friends. He lied. He wasn't ready to tell him about the night.

Bronwyn came out a bit later, standing beneath the eaves of the little house, watching the storm as it blew across the night sky.

"We can't leave it there," Josh said. "It's loose now. You think the cops will believe us? You think anyone will?"

For just a moment, she looked empty. That's the best way he thought of it. She looked as if there was nothing to her at all. All she wanted to do was get away. Even from him. She just wanted to run in the opposite direction, even if it meant that Scratch was going to be hunting others.

"Go on," he said. "You can call your dad. Get him to wire you money. Rent a car or catch a bus. And go on. But it's out there. I can't just go back to life and forget that. What if campers go out there? What if, at night, a policeman shows up to look at the cars? What if Scratch is just waiting for them?"

Her shoulders went slack.

"Tomorrow morning, go. I don't blame you."

She didn't blink. She wasn't going to stay behind; he saw it in her eyes. "I think you should come, too. You're not obligated to deal with that thing. It's a monster, Josh. We can get help. We can . . ."

"Nope. I think there's a way to stop it. I think there's a way to end this. I need to try something."

"I don't want you . . ." she began. He knew how that sentence finished: to die.

"We all die, Bron. We die. Life is a short space of time. Some people die young, some die at middle age, some die old. We're lucky if it's swift. We're lucky if it's only seconds of pain. We're lucky if what's between when we're born and when we die is a powerful thing. A miraculous thing. I never believed in miracles. Before. I never believed that the goodness of the universe existed. But I know it does. I don't believe for a minute that we've gone through this night because life is horrible. Or because monsters rule. Or because we're meant to. I believe this is a test. This is a test, and to pass it, to find out who each of us truly is, we have to stand up to this thing. We have to stop it. Because not stopping it is just letting the bad things happen. For me, not stopping it is worse than getting killed."

"You're going to die out there. Oh, please, Josh. Please. Don't be the next victim."

"I am not going to sacrifice myself," Josh said. "I know I can stop it. I know it. Here's how I was living before this, Bron: I was living as if nothing mattered. As if life were a joke. As if it didn't matter whether I was happy or sad, or did nothing or did something. I was on disconnect. But last night showed me. Life is about something. We are about something. I am. And I know I can stop it."

"Please don't die," she said, quietly. Calmly. "Don't be some kind of hero."

"I'm going to do what I know I have to do," he said. "We woke that thing up. I have to put it back to sleep."

7

He bought the little souvenir at a shop in downtown Naga. Ely loaned him his busted-up Civic, and Josh drove around trying to gather what he thought might help. He went to the library in Naga and read a little in the reference section. He felt foolish and doomed, but something inside him—some engine—had begun to turn over. Something had changed within him from that one night.

The rain continued into his second evening at Ely's. Bronwyn had already gotten on a bus headed for Los Angeles, and although she told him she loved him, he knew now that it wasn't love. It was simply attraction and situation. Love was something else. He hoped to have it someday, but it wasn't a feeling you could hand over to someone. It was deeper than that. He wished her the best, kissed her good-bye, and he told her that he would stop Scratch so that no one else would ever get hurt.

He sat down with Ely and told him everything except the truth. Josh refused to let another person—either friend or foe—die because they'd let Scratch out of its cage.

157

8

He withdrew what he'd bought the day before.

Probably not an authentic Native American design, but it looked real enough.

Tourist crap, no doubt.

The stone was carved to a point.

An arrowhead.

Made out of obsidian.

Obsidian was the translucent dark stone used in the Aztec ritual.

The dagger went into the heart. Something like that. He wasn't sure how it was done. But the heart was brought up, spraying blood.

How the Flayer of Men, the Flesh-Scraper, then skinned the bodies. And wore the skin.

Obsidian was sacred.

It had magical properties.

And even the avatar of Xipe Totec, Mr. Scratch, would have something resembling a heart. Some engine that ran him.

Sure, Josh thought. *Maybe it was all roadside attraction mumbo-jumbo. Mystical babble that some con artist had written up to get tourist dollars off the highway.*

He held the arrowhead in his hand. It felt cool against his hot skin.

Please. I don't believe in anything other than the goodness of the universe. Let it be here. Let it be with me now. Give me the strength to stop this abomination.

Without even knowing why, Josh fell to his knees, clutching the arrowhead. He closed his eyes.

Whatever I have in me. Whatever there is beside flesh and blood and molecules and nerves and bone. Let it come out in me. Let it come through me. In the name of Griff and Ziggy and Tammy and Dave. And that other guy.

Dave's friend.

In the name of them, and their memories. Their lives. Their life forces.

And my own.

Give me the power.

The knowledge.

The ability.

To stop this creature.

9

Josh drove back up the road that ended, and found the Pimpmobile. The rain had stopped hours ago. The sun beat down on his scalp and the back of his neck. He got up after a bit, feeling slightly dizzy. He went down and sat under a manzanilla tree—a gathering of bleached sticks more than a tree, but it provided a very slight shade. He drew down one of the dried branches and began creating the weapon.

Within a few hours, it looked good.

The arrowhead was tied—with a strip from his belt, which he'd shredded—and the tree branch was smooth and white—an imperfect spear.

He tried throwing it, but his aim sucked. He

felt weak and sleepy, and knew he needed to rest if he were to fight in the darkness.

So he slept, using his shirt and jeans as a bit of a tent, propped up between rocks and sticks and scrub.

It was boiling, but at least for a bit, the bright searing eye of the sun was not upon him.

His dreams came fast and feverish—

They were dragging him up the long steps, up the pyramid. Only it wasn't a real pyramid. It was like a cartoon. It was like someone had made it up, and hastily drawn the stones and the men who dragged him—everything was all outline, with no substance.

They stood over him—Ziggy, Griff, and Tammy—and held him down against a freezing cold stone. Above him, the face of Charlie Goodrow, from the gas station. Their big greasy mugs looked down at him, while someone else raised a shiny black knife just over his head.

When it thrust down, he screamed. Charlie Goodrow brought up a big mass of pulsating red, and started crowing, "He's a gusher! Lookit that! The boy gushes like a goddamn sweet Texas oil field."

Josh's blood sprayed up, peppering their faces, splashing their features until all of them were red. Josh thrashed, wanted his heart back, but felt no real pain.

Someone began playing some kind of reed instrument, and a drum was beaten slowly. A woman's voice began singing a strange, un-melodic song.

Although it was in another language, Josh knew what it meant:

Flayer of Men
Bring us your rainfall
We give you blood
Bring us life!
We offer flesh for scraping
To you alone—
Flayer of Men
Dance in his skin
Dance so that children may be born!
Dance so that the crops will grow!
Dance so that the sun will not burn your people!
Dance and be reborn in blood and life, from your dark place!

And then Josh became disembodied, floating along the flat but rough stone floor within the pyramid, lit by torch, and watched as the Flayer of Men scraped the skin using the long needle-like talons, carefully drawing the top layer of flesh from the meat, and pressing it, with blood still dripping, against his shadowy face.

Josh drew closer to look at the eyes of the scraper, but they were empty sockets, and Josh realized that he was looking at his own skin, laid across the Flesh-Scraper's small body, wrapped and sewn together.

The Flayer began to move oddly, side to side—
a dance of life and death, wearing the skin of the
sacrifice.

Suddenly, Josh no longer watched this dance,
but was inside, behind the skin, looking out.

10

He awoke.

It was night.

He sat up, feeling the dryness at his lips and
the scaly feeling in his throat.

11

He waited a long time, until he heard the scraping sound.

The only light was the luminescence of the
white sand of the desert, the enormous blue-faded
moon in the sky, and the stars, which, as he looked
up at them, seemed to him so far away as to be un-
concerned with the problems of a man of nineteen
in the middle of a wasteland waiting for a monster.

12

The gasping sound came first, then the sound of
something being dragged.

Against the whiteness, he saw a small dark form.

Running between bits of brush and clutches of
cactus.

He felt a lump form in his throat. He wondered whether a person could genuinely die of fright.

13

He knew Scratch's hunting method now. He knew that the little mummy liked to get the scares going. It was its ritual. Get the scares going, make a big to-do, get people on the edge of their seats, and then strike.

He felt his nerves jangling, and wondered whether prey animals felt this just before an eagle or owl swooped down, or a mountain lion neared.

He felt like prey, and it brought with it that strange sensation he'd felt before:

That somehow he was more alive now. That this monster, this evil, horrible thing, could somehow make him more aware of every cell in his body, right down to his toes and the electrical whirring beneath the skin of his fingers.

14

And as he sat there, thinking all this, feeling it, he felt the first scrape of talon along his ankle.

He reached back for his weapon.

The obsidian arrowhead, tied to the nearly smooth stick.

The hunt had begun.

Chapter Thirteen

1

A second scrape at his ankle took away an outer layer of skin. Bleeding. Hurt like hell. But he leapt up and circled around, feeling like a hunter in some ancient world, holding the spear up.

"Come on, Scratch," he said. His voice was raspy.

He could not see anything other than shapes against the earth.

He wasn't sure if he had begun imagining things, but it seemed like there were several shapes moving—shadows against shadows.

I'm losing it.

2

Make me a warrior. Make me a man. Make me the hero. Make me the one. It was like a chant in his head. *Fill me with strength. Give me power over my enemies. I am good. I am just. I will overcome. I will defeat. I will be the victor.*

As he circled the car, then wandered a ways into the dark, holding the spear up, he felt . . . tribal. He felt connected. He had a welling within him that made him feel as if he were not fighting some monster on the desert, but participating in some ancient rite of manhood—that he was meant to be here. Gone were the trappings of home and university and his sense of the future and his hold on the past.

He was HUNTER.

He was HUNTER and this thing was his HUNTED.

I AM NOT PREY! I AM NOT PREY! You are rabbit. I am coyote. You are serpent! I am eagle! I AM THE HUNTER OF THE GODS OF DEATH!

3

A lightening of his being occurred—he no longer felt the small jabs of rock beneath his feet, nor did he feel the fear, nor did the desert seem as dark.

He felt as if a weight had been lifted from him and cast off into shadows.

And there it was.

The Being.

The Creature.

The Flayer of Men.

He knew its name. Its ritual name.

Xipe Totec! You are under my foot!
Xipe Totec! You are the skin of the snake!
Xipe Totec! You have no power of me!
I am the PRIEST and the HUNTER of Death.

A small voice within him: *Am I mad? Is this insanity?*

But the larger voice within him—the voice of a man he barely recognized—said aloud, "I am here to destroy you!"

4

His voice seemed to come from a different place inside him. Something had been awakened.

5

The creature leapt at him, and he lost his balance, falling backward. The spear went flying back, out of his reach.

He felt the claws dig in—Scratch was crawling up along his left leg. The pain was excruciating.

I'm not afraid of pain. I will not be afraid of pain. Pain is nothing. Pain is a scream to nowhere. Pain is meaningless.

He felt as if the veins of his legs were being ripped out, but he gritted his teeth and refused to accept the agony.

I AM THE PRIEST. I AM THE HUNTER.

6

It tugged at his legs, and began dragging him across the rocks and sand. His head hit the back of a rock, and he felt himself lose consciousness.

I AM THE PRIEST.

I AM.

7

Hang on. Hang on. This is no dream. This is real. Wake up. Wake up.

Josh opened his eyes. He felt blood pumping within him. *I am alive. I am alive. I will not die.* He pivoted on his hips as Scratch drew him across the dirt. Then he reached out and dug his fingernails down into the earth. Pressed his fingers in. Held on.

The screaming pain in his calves was intense.

The talons had gone in deep. He wasn't sure how much blood he'd lost.

He dug his other hand into the dirt. Hurt like razors.

He groped in the dirt and tugged himself back. Maybe a quarter inch. Glanced in the darkness. Manzanilla. Rocks. Car. He dragged himself farther. Toward the spear. Toward the obsidian arrowhead.

He couldn't be certain, but he thought he saw

the makeshift spear lying just out of his grasp.

Scratch was chewing on his left leg, but if he tried—if he took all he had—he could get the spear. Something was drawing him down into a dark maelstrom in his head, but he dragged himself forward.

Touched the edge of the spear. His hand went around it. He drew it back, and sat up.

He thought he saw the look on Scratch's face, as the turquoise eyes stared at him.

He brought the spear down into Scratch's jaw, and then pulled hard on it until he heard a crack. At first, he thought the spear had broken, but it was the creature's lower jaw that fell sideways, hanging by a small bit of gristle.

Josh drew the spear out, putting his hand close to where the obsidian was wrapped around the base.

He plunged the arrowhead into the space beneath Scratch's breastbone.

Scratch's claws curled around his fingers.

"You can't kill me," Scratch said with Tammy's voice, but it was funny-sounding as its dangling jaw wagged. "You know that. You know all about me, don't you? Give yourself to Xipe Totec! Heroes must be sacrificed."

But, in fact, just as Josh had suspected, the mummy had some kind of moist pulpy material within its ribcage: a beating heart, perhaps not like a human heart, but a heart nonetheless.

And the obsidian went into it.

The claws let go of his wrist.

Josh drew the arrowhead up.

At its tip, a mass of bloody tissue.

The great Flayer of Men lay still at his bloody legs.

At some point, Josh passed out.

8

When he awoke, someone was pouring cool water over him.

Josh opened his eyes. Early daylight.

A large, thickset man with a day's growth of beard sat beside him. In his hand, a large bottle of Poland Spring Water.

"Ely?"

Josh glanced around. Ely was carefully lifting him up to get in the truck with him. "Hello, kid. I was pretty sure you were a goner."

"My legs . . ."

"Yeah, I saw 'em. Torn up real bad. Mountain lion?"

Josh didn't respond.

"You're some kind of superman, kid. Lost a lot of blood. I saw you just crawling by the road there. Let's get you over to the hospital. They can patch you up. I suck at it. Look, don't talk. We'll get there soon enough. Can you hang on?"

Josh nodded. He took the bottle of water from Ely's hand and drank from it.

He felt the rumble of the truck start up.

"You kill the lion?"

"What?"

"The mountain lion. That attacked you. You kill it?"

"Not sure," Josh said. "I hurt it. I know that."

"Well, that's something," Ely said. He got the truck in gear and pulled back out on the highway. "It's something to put a hurt back on a beast like that. When you're all better, I want you to tell me everything you didn't tell me, okay?"

Chapter Fourteen

1

And that's when I became a man. My name is Joshua, and I've grown to love this desert. All that happened a long time ago, before the new highway came in, before I moved permanently to Naga, Arizona, and before I began to understand my place in the world. I dropped out of college, went to live in that small town where Ely had dropped me, and a few years after wallowing in misery and guilt and alcohol, met my wife, lived my life. I got work as a writer and worked at a bookstore in town, but I didn't last long in many jobs.

2

I went back, after I'd plunged the razor-sharp obsidian in that monster's heart. After my legs healed. After some time had passed and I could face it again.

I wanted to examine it before destroying it. In size, it was four feet four inches tall, and while I didn't weigh it, I can guess it was about sixty pounds. The gauze on its body—what kept its bones wrapped—was not what I had expected. I had assumed it was some kind of cloth, but, instead, it was fine, thin layers of human skin, torn into strips, wrapped around the bone of the creature. I held up one of its claws. Each talon was its own blade, and was razor-sharp.

I plucked the turquoise from its eyes, because I'd been reading about rituals by then. It could be blinded. It could be incapacitated.

The more I looked at it, the more I began to feel for it. What is it in human life that does it? That holds a monster in its arms and feels something like kinship—an instinct to care and protect? A demon, sleeping, in my arms, seemed vulnerable and in need, to me.

I placed it inside a leather-bound box lined with stone, closing Scratch up inside it, its coffin. If no one fed it again, if no one let it out, surely, it could just sleep forever.

And in sleeping, what damage could this thing do?

In the meantime, I began reading more about ancient ritual. I got odd jobs, and then, after my parents died, I inherited a lump sum of cash, and spent much of it on ordering books from around the world. I wanted to know more about this—the invisible world around us, the monsters, the gods, the creatures of legend. I wanted to understand this "it" until I began to see "it" as "him."

One night, troubled by fears, I went out to the furthest mesa, and buried him deep, the way I'd bury something toxic, something that no man should ever touch, ever know.

But the cities and towns are growing. They're taking over parts of the desert that had once been vast wastelands, miles of nothing.

Now suburban homes are being built on the mesa, and the bulldozers dig down deep to lay foundations and carve out swimming pools. Scorpions swarm as they're sent from their nests. Rattlesnakes are killed by workmen who find them under nearly every rock.

I didn't mark the place where I buried Scratch. I didn't put a flag over it so I could see where it was.

I buried it to end it, to forget it, to put the demon somewhere it would never be found.

But I was wrong.

They're digging all over that mesa. They'll find him. They'll bring him out. Maybe they already have.

The Flayer of Men will dance, and this time, I may not be able to stop it. I will try to understand Scratch. To try to keep him from doing what his nature compels him to do.

I may not have enough skin on me to keep that thing from running wild. There may not be enough obsidian blades to stop its beating heart.

They say a rainstorm's on the way.

THE NECROMANCER

A novella of Harrow

*Being the Diary of Justin Gravesend
on the Year of his Rebirth,
and his forced initiation
into the Chymera Magick,
including his early visionaries.*

*For Melisse, a story of debauchery and darkness for you,
and a borrowed name.*

To be shared with M.J. Rose.

Somnia, terrores magicos, miracula, fagas, nocturnos lemures, portentaques . . .

—Horace

All places shall be hell that is not heaven.
—Christopher Marlowe, *Dr. Faustus*

A Brief Note from Douglas Clegg

The early tales of Harrow are drawn from diaries and fragments of diaries, for the most part. This diary of Justin Gravesend's early life is one of several he kept during his lifetime. Additionally, he encouraged the keeping of diaries by his wife and mistresses when he was an older man, no doubt to enhance whatever fame or delusions of grandeur he had.

What is perhaps most remarkable, to me, was the discovery of poem fragments in this diary. I include with this document an introduction by an esteemed academician whose primary studies have been in the history of the occult and classical mythology. Additionally, I have placed Gravesend's so-called "Visionaries" in the order in which he had set them, on separate sheets of parchment, within the diary itself, as if place markers of some sort.

Introduction from a student of the Necromancer's Diary

As someone who researches the arcane and unusual artifacts of mystical significance, I chanced upon this diary purely by accident while researching a series of grisly murders that occurred in London in the mid-1800s. These were lesser-known killings than the more famous Whitechapel murders attributed to one Jack the Ripper decades later. My hunch as to why these murders did not become better known is that the authorities did not know what to make of them, given the condition of the bodies, and because there was the hint of scandal of an upper-class sort around them (for four of the victims were eventually identified), that it was kept quiet in all but the highest circles. There is also the peculiar nature of their discovery: The six victims included two young men of good family, two women, also of good family. They had been entirely eviscerated, their facial features obliterated so that it was difficult if not impossible in some cases to identify them, and on their bodies, occult symbols and monstrous creatures had been tattooed, to the extent that not an inch was left that was not somehow painted over with the tattoo. In going over papers at Scotland Yard, in their historic records library, I learned of the existence of this diary, or rather a fragment of the diary, and, through a series of collectors, managed to purchase a photocopy of it, which I'm reprinting here. Some of the pages were illegible or drawn over with symbols and a language I could not precisely translate, if it was anything more than nonsense.

The nature of a diary is not toward narrative. It is an accounting of events, generally in order. Certain unnecessary sections have been eliminated, including Gravesend's obsessive bookkeeping, house accounting, as well as his sketches and diagrams of both the human body and of fantastical machines that are his ideas, apparently, of how to either torture a human being, or how to drill into the earth. The stuff of science fiction novels or pornography. This diary in your hands is slightly different, for there is something of a narrative to it, although this utterly falls apart in its latter half. It is not about order, but about disorder, and this seemed to speak to the state of mind of its author. If we are to believe there is some truth to Gravesend's grand conspiracy, of

Watchers who follow his moves and direct him to his fateful destination, we would give in to the madness that was Gravesend himself. As you perhaps have read from other books written about the man, he was "the most evil man in existence," or at least that is what the newspapers called him, when he held his famous "Summoning Demons" parties of the late 1800s at his magnificent estate called Harrow. We must understand a little of Gravesend in his later life to put this account of his youth into context.

While Gravesend died in the mid-1920s, outliving his own son, he was not a well-known personage of his time, except among occult circles, and I suspect he enjoyed keeping it that way. In his younger years, he had some fame, primarily from claiming that he was bringing what he called the Age of Baphomet into the world through spiritual endeavors and gatherings that read like a Who's Who of the occult world. (This information can easily be found in the other books related to Gravesend, including the famous memoir, *The Oracle* by the mysterious Isis Claviger, a clairvoyant of the early twentieth century who claimed to be the reincarnation of one of Gravesend's first human sacrifices. She also claimed she was a reincarnation of Astarte, a priestess of the ancient world who was the mythic founder of the Chymera Magick and of the flower called herein "Lotos.")

What is remarkable is that at such a young age,

he was willing to keep record of these grisly and immoral goings-on of his early life. That he was willing to write down the secrets of this legendary group, the Chymera Magick, and at least a fragment of its initiation rituals, which primarily have to do with sex and murder.

A note on the Chymera Magick: This was an order of occultists whose aim is unknown, but which claimed to have originated in Egyptian and Greek Mystery religions combined with a shoddy alchemy and sense of Black Magic, in the nineteenth-century mystical way of thinking of it. Stealing slightly from the Cabala and the Eastern traditions, as well as from the medieval sense of witchcraft and divination, the Chymera Magick seemed to disband in 1914. I believe it merely went further underground. The infamous book of the Chymerians (as they called themselves) has never been recovered, although Gravesend refers to it within this mishmash of a diary that seems half-brag of his sexual exploits and half-delight in the horror of his devilry. The Grimoire Chymera, as it is called, is most likely a fabrication.

The stories surrounding the Grimoire Chymera were many. Some believed they had the ability to change shape within a range of creatures: to a wolf, to a raven, to serpent. Or the ability to change between man and woman and back again. The language, or as the Chymerians had it, "The Words," of something called The Veil of the Profane, a place reached with something akin to the opium pipe with the extract of a plant they simply called "Lotos." While we don't know what plant this is, there is a good chance that Gravesend and his fellow Chymerians were simply "chasing the dragon" in opium dens, which were popular during much of his life. Additionally, there was the usual—and nearly hackneyed—idea of changing base metals to gold, of acquiring wealth through the mental and magnetic enslavement of others of lesser will. They had maps of the ancient, buried world wherein occult treasures could be found. The key to all mystical texts also supposedly could be found in the Grimoire Chymera: the code of the Bible, the genuine translation of the sayings of Jesus, the spells within the epic of Gilgamesh, among other items lesser known today. The Grimoire also contained the exact formula for gravity defiance, that individual human flight could be possible with the application of a salve on the skin and a long bout of meditation. Purportedly, there was a way to become briefly invisible, to murder someone by simply kissing him on the neck, and to read the minds of the weakest among humankind in order to have dominion over them. There was also a section in this book that went into the thousand names of the gods, and why mankind had lost the ability to speak directly to them.

It is a grand mythos that the Chymera Magick introduced through their circle, and it is my guess that they duped many of their members into believing that they were something more than a fraternity of murder, greed, and sexual licentiousness.

More specifically, the life of Justin Gravesend began and ended in his twenty-first year when he left school and his uncle-benefactor. Justin went down to London, where he first met the man who would be his Mage, his Guide, his Master through his initiation into the Chymera Magick. He refers to this man only as The Necromancer, giving him no Christian name whatsoever, and by this title we know him, and have no idea what further exploits this Necromancer may have had. The Necromancer is obviously a bisexual deviant, someone who finds greatest gratification in perversion, and who is very likely, by the standards of his day, a sadist in the tradition of the writings of the Marquis de Sade (of which, no doubt, Justin and his contemporaries knew well.) While the Necromancer has his share of young women, in a Casanova-like style, he seems peculiarly attracted to men, using them for what he called "Sex Magick," which seems to be none other than sexual deviancy disguised as a transformative experience.

Certainly, young Justin Gravesend came under his tutelage and experienced what he considered orgiastic visions. But we must remember that these are the words of a young man, experimenting with narcotics and sex and what he calls "the disordering of the senses" through violence.

"Awaking the sleeping beast" is his other phrase, and seems to be a philosophy of the Chymerians in general.

It will be of note that this diary merely ends. It does not reach a satisfactory conclusion, and it is perhaps the beginning of a second diary that Gravesend might've kept. We know of his life after his twenty-first year. He became a captain of industry, a robber baron of sorts, and then retired early to build his greatest creation, the house known as Harrow up the Hudson River of New York. Despite amassing great wealth and building an estate of considerable proportions after his time with the Necromancer, Gravesend seemed to enter a quiet period of his life. In his thirties, he married, raised a child, and although other legends have been connected to the man and his home, he seemed to have settled down in much the same way that young people everywhere settle down to a life of comparable normalcy. By the age of forty-six, he was entirely retired, living as landed gentry at Harrow. In the 1920s, Gravesend died, having outlived his own son. The house went to his grandson, and then to someone outside the family named Alfred Barrow, who eventually turned it into, and sold it off as, a school. When the school shut down, it went through at least two more ownerships, dogged as any architectural madness might be by legends of crime and murder and haunting. (I visited the grounds of Harrow in late 2002, although it is now completely closed off from the road with razor wire and ugly chain link fences, a blight on the natural beauty of the area surrounding it, like a pre-Berlin Wall Checkpoint Charlie.)

I have tried to track down the real person who is behind the title Necromancer, but so far my pursuit has been unsuccessful. I did locate more about one particular player in his drama, the little girl named Isis, who later become a psychic and a writer on the supernatural world and its exploration. In the diary, she is an enigma to Gravesend and to any who read about her. But I know there are other documents that will tell me more about her.

One final note: the city referred to as Nuvo Cartigius, or New Carthage, is obviously not on any map, nor does there seem to be an island off Greece that corresponds to its greater location. Most likely, this is a gathering place for the Chymerians, perhaps a villa of sorts on one of those small, unremarkable islands among the larger ones in the Mediterranean Sea. I will provide a brief glossary at the end of this printed form of the diary for those who are new to the Chymera Magick and its occult terms.

One thing the sharp reader will notice is that, despite his writing in the 1800s, Gravesend seems to have a twentieth-century perspective on his adventures. This has led more than one scholar (see Emil Marquand's thesis, presented to the Prague International Occult Congress, 2000, on "The Occult Elite in America and England: 1850–1900") to postulate that Gravesend himself did not write the diary at the time he experienced it, but perhaps dictated it to a secretary of some sort when he was an older man. While this seemingly moot point can be ignored, it is a possibility of which to be aware while reading of these miscreant and diabolical (in the classical sense) adventures.

Editor's Note: Owing to Gravesend's lack of precise dates for his diary entries, we have taken it upon ourselves to divide the diary into chapters for easier divisions of events and occurrences. The so-called "Visionaries," as Gravesend called his drug-induced dreams, are set off as their own subsections. These were a mishmash of notes, nearly poems, which should not be taken at face value as I believe they were Gravesend's poetic mysticism, more savage than Blake's, perhaps, but similar in that they are to be taken as fantasies—often sexual—of a disturbed and possibly addicted mind. We did not set them down in any particular order. Although they are number 1, 2, 3, etc., they were gathered in piles, torn from other notebooks, included here as an illumination of the state of mind of Justin Gravesend in his youth.

—James Wandigaux, Ph.D., Professor Emeritus,
The College of Arts and Sciences, Rutherford
University, Surrey, New York

PART ONE

A ddarlenno, ysteried
(Translated from the Welsh: *Let him who reads, reflect.*)

The magician must stand in the posture of supplication, lifting the sacrifice from the field of time into the great sea beyond the Veil, ensuring that the six great pleasures are enacted with regard to the energy points, and the openings are sealed with flesh. Thereby shall he ask nothing of the devourers that he would not ask of himself, and there shall he offer the meat with praise and thanksgiving, for the meat is the life of the devourers, and without meat, there is no sacrifice, and without sacrifice, there is no transformation . . .

—*The Grimoire Chymera*

Behold, the architecture of your life
Alive, in these bones
Passing into my hands
How you speak to me of Tyre and Sodom!
O, sound the ram's horn of Jericho's passing!
Make the heavens shake, and below, the Devils cry!
Each man must die, each city fall
To kiss our Mother Death, laughing, in her pall.
            —Justin Gravesend, from *Mother Death Speaks*

Visionary 1

She slams my head back against the wall and holds her hand against my chest, pushing down upon the area above my heart, tearing at the slender hairs around my nipple, her spit landing on my eye as I slap her as hard as I can across her face and reach for her hair, pulling it back as hard as I can; I manage to roll on top of her and cover her biting mouth with my gloved hand, and when I let go, she cries out, "Yes, please, yes, yes, sweet, sweet," and then I feel the building of the orgiastic light as waves of undiluted pleasure, set free from conscience, rise within me, within me and my willing partner; she is going there with me, she is giving herself to our destination, and I press myself into her opening flower, holding myself there for the count of one, two, three, four, five, and then the Veil opens before my eyes, and for the first time I see the creature with the three mouths and the fingers like talons, and in its eyes, a feral kindness, like the wolf-cub found in the woods, and I watch, as if floating in the air before it, as it spreads its seven translucent wings and tears greedily into the offered sacrifice.

It wants the throat.

The sacrifice turns her head slightly, to offer.

Her throat is a delight; it is a torment; it is meat.

It is the first milk from a mother, the first taste of life.

Chapter One

My First Birth and Family

1

I was told that the night I was born, my mother saw a terrible face at the window of the midwife's house, of a man who seemed the very devil.

Given that I have spent most of my life in the devil's shadow, I believe my mother saw the truth.

2

I was born a monster, and I grew from a monstrous life, and if you read of this, you will understand. I had no choice in my monstrosity.

Fate takes us by the hand and leads us where we are meant to go, and, in turn, we bite her for the pleasure of it. I am a murderer and a scoundrel, but once, I was a child, just as you once have been. Once I sought the goodness of all creation.

Once, I was a common urchin in a tidal pool, surrounded by eagerly devouring eels.

It is all a charade! This life! How we see it! How I saw my own! My life was never my own, but was drawn up as if by a great draughtsman, this Necromancer who had found the relics and used them to enslave me and bring me into the Veil!

I should have burned my books and instead turned to the quiet rustic life to which I had been born, and died with coal-dust in my throat and seven babies 'round the room, and a wife at the hearth! Instead, I allowed the curse that had been laid upon me at the hour of my birth to grow and fester. I followed my will, my flesh, and those who guided me, to this most wondrous and terrible place! Read this and know!

I have seen the other side of existence and it has torn away all conscience from me, and yet, I love the horror more than I love life itself and would not turn back if given the choice.

3

Pleasure and its humours in the human body are what allow us to experience the mystical world. My first pleasure was my mother's nipple and my last, in my twenty-first year, was found at the breast of the Whore of Babylon, that visionary salve, that nectar of the necropolis, the supreme Lotos of the Visionary.

Why me? We each cry, alone, to the universe, to

the mute gods or God. Why this fate? Why my destiny and not the destiny of the comfortable life, free of terror and abominations of the flesh? Why not the hypocritical, cushioned life of the normal man? Why not the world in which God is for Sundays and life consists of hours of labor followed by a few hours of entertainment and rest? Why this soul searing?

This I cannot answer satisfactorily. I was chosen before I even knew a choice could be made. My only answer can be that it was destiny itself, carved on my bones and sung within the chambers of my heart.

I had a sponsor to bring me to the attention of that secret society called the Chymera Magick. I could not have avoided my destiny had I desired to do so.

My life is written on my skin, tattooed as surely as if needles had been pressed into me, in the pathways of my blood and the subcutaneous layers, the prick of life—and of the Occult Arts— dug chigger-like into me, and it is there. We are not mind, although we feel we are. We are body, we are flesh, we are the points of hair and the torn skin, and it is the obliteration of the mind that brings us in contact with the visions and the truth. It is through the destruction of social hypocrisy, of taboo, of restraint. This opens us up, finds doorways where there have been none. This bores holes into us, opening us to the vibrant hum of the cosmos. In the story of my life, you will read of terrible things, by your standards. You will read of vows broken, of demons raised, of bodies used unnaturally, of deviancy and unholy ritual, of nuns brought into the orgy pit, and of men used as women, and women used as men. Do not flinch from this, for that is the squint of the weak human mind we believe we possess.

Use these shocking acts as a way of awakening the creature within its cage.

The one who is the Many. The Lord of the Flies is no devil. The Lord of Pestilence is no beekeeper of souls.

He is our brother.

Use this to gain wisdom and seek your heaven. I have seen the afterworld, and I will tell you it is more terrible than the worst tortures of this fair land. Do you walk the Earth and believe it unmerciful and unjust? The life beyond this one is ten thousand times more horrible. It is a screaming moment frozen in an eternal chamber of torment. You would do well to seek the disordering of your senses now, to ungird yourselves of your weighty prison of the mind and unleash every desire of your flesh, every forbidden thing you can imagine, let it come to pass. For the end of your life already circles around you. You shall be bitten by its ravening silver teeth, and torn by its pincers. You must embrace it and open yourself to it.

As I did.

4

I came into the world feeling as if something important had been taken from me. And it is this, more than my want of wealth and power and happiness, which has driven me to my current state.

My name is Justin Gravesend, although this was not my name at birth.

Then, I was named Iestyn, a Welsh form of Justin, meaning, of course, "the just." It was an old-fashioned name to have when I was a boy, but it was a relief to avoid the Biblical names that were so popular then. I was born near an ancient colliery and its spoil heaps, in operation since the Middle Ages, which seemed fitting since it was its own kind of torture chamber. The coalfields were the dark heart of all our existences, with the wool industry taking second place. The village where I grew up was small then, called Cwthshire, pronounced Coo-shire, and our nearest city, a good forty miles away, was called Llangolen, and even that was not much of a city then. I am sorry to say that our little village no longer exists, abandoned when the local mining ended with several explosions that killed many miners and closed off the mine itself.

When I was a child, it was my kingdom.

We lived near three rivers, one wide and broad that ran through the village, tamed as a canal before my birth, called the Range for a reason I never have understood, and two slimmer ones that seemed mere streams to me as a boy. I did not speak Welsh well, owing in part to the fact that my parents both discouraged it. We were not really a Welsh family, although my father's Welshness-by-way-of-Manchester-and-Liverpool existed in much the same way as my mother's slight Irishness: in a few names, a few phrases, and not much else. They had arrived in Cwthshire to find work and life in the colliery and the sheep meadows. My mother was Catholic, from Ireland by way of Scotland by way of Cornwall. My father was Methodist. He had been born in Wales and was taken to Liverpool while a child. He had grown to hate all things English and all things about his father and brothers. He had come to the mines and fields for work, young. He had adopted the harsh local church's ways to such an extent that the locals called him Deacon, and on Sundays, would give fire and brimstone speeches, nearly stealing the pulpit from the local minister.

He believed that hell lay in wait for all of us, for we had been baptized in what he called "The Devil's pagan church," his term for the Roman Catholic Church. He was certain that we all would die without resurrection, and that our mother, whom he claimed to love dearly, had already lost her mortal soul to the fires of hell, but that his good Christian nature tried to redeem her throughout their lives together. He believed that heaven was harder to get into than the local pub on a Saturday night. He typified the Welsh phrase: *Angel pen ffordd, a diawl pen tan. An angel abroad, a devil at home.*

Whereas he was an inspiration to the local congregation and considered one of the great local men of God (on Sundays, although he was well-ignored by the villagers the rest of the time), he was a cold, hard taskmaster to his children.

He used God to squelch us, and the threat of hell to keep us silent. He continued his Methodist traditions within our family and had named the first five of my siblings biblically. Thus, I had brothers Shadrac, Mishac, and Abednego, and sisters Sephera and Bathsheba. I had escaped this fate when my mother insisted on naming me for her grandfather, who had recently died, and my twin, for my father's father.

My father's family was called ap Graver or sometimes Graver-Son (or Son of Graver, as my birth record reads: "Baptized this day, July, Iestyn, son of the Son of Graver"), and was from the ancient and country people, with peasants and yeomen in our ancestry, of Wales mixed with the conquering English. My father was a fallen son of a fallen son. This meant he had cousins and even brothers who had some wealth, but through a series of bad events, my father had no contact with them. He had been slothful (I can truthfully write now, but I could never think this when living under his roof), and had believed that one ought not to work for one's daily bread, but must convince others to pass their bread over for his convenience. My father, unlike my brothers and me, never worked the mines or the field. He was not a laborer, my mother would tell us, as she worked in peoples' homes and swept the alleyways behind the shops to make the pittance that supported all of us. My father was a ne'er-do-well, and not of the romantic variety. His face was like a crazed eagle—the nose hooked, the eyes blue, the nostrils flared, and the filthy mop of hair across his forehead like some overgrown barley field.

My mother was a martyr who refused to die—she lived through the deaths of four of her children. She worked any job she could find, still managed to say the rosary at the local church twice a day, and believed that Jesus Christ and the Virgin Mary had given her these burdens in order to prepare her for sainthood in the next life. I honestly believe she wanted to die and be remembered for her Faith. Instead, the poor woman—whom I loved dearly, despite my talk of her—lived until she was ninety-three, and saw all she loved destroyed, and all she feared, come to pass.

I was born when she was thirty-six, and my father was forty. My earliest memory is looking up at my mother's face, as I, at three, was still at her tit, nursing. She looked like the Virgin Mother to me then, and I remembered being disappointed when I could no longer drink that sacred milk.

In my generation was the beginning of my re-generation. In my father's loins and my mother's womb, a mystery arrived to the world. I was not that mystery, but I was born with it. I was born in the year 1831, during a cholera epidemic, which was then simply called the Miasma. According to legend (for I heard of it years later), the Miasma swept through like a broom from hell ("A scourge!" my father shouted from the pulpit, no doubt), taking with it the breath of many children in ours and other villages. The cities beyond us also were in its path, and many died during this time, particularly among the very young and the very old.

Mother Death (as the locals called her) spared me.

As I grew, I seemed to develop a taste for the morbid, and often went to the graveyard of the children who had died, feeling as if I somehow knew them better than the children who were alive. I can't say for certain that this came from any particular event. It was simply something about death that drew me to it, rather than repulsed me.

My mother later told me the hand of God was upon me, and protected me from the Miasma.

But God was nowhere to be found for my twin. When I learned of his name and his death, I wept and was inconsolable. I had always felt a strange emptiness, as if I were only half a boy, as if I had another part of me that was somehow missing, as one is missing an arm or a leg—a phantom self

that I had knowledge of, but knew not. It is difficult to express, but it was like knowing that one
isn't completely alive. A lung that does not function. A nostril that cannot inhale and exhale
breath. I felt that my brothers and sisters and
friends in the mines and in the schoolhouse, all
seemed whole. But I did not. And when my
mother told me about my dead twin, I knew why.

My twin died six months after we were born.
His name was Lloyd. I visited his little grave in
the field beyond the village, sometimes weekly,
and thought of how close I had gotten to Mother
Death, but she had instead chosen to suckle my
brother. I sometimes attribute my need for "the
Other" and some of the unsuitable attachments
I've made in my life to the loss of that unknowable twin.

My only experience with the spirit world as a
child came while I sat by my twin's grave. I
wasn't then sure of what it meant, if it was anything at all. I just heard someone say the words,
"Carry me to the water, look, and know the
truth."

5

Carry me to the water? Know the truth? These
words seemed too profound to have come just
from my childish mind.

And yet, more than anything, I wanted to
know. I wanted to know my twin in some way. I

wanted to understand what, even then, I considered a mystical experience.

I went to my older sister Bathsheba, who was my only true confidante among my siblings. She was sixteen, and ready to be married, and in some ways had been more my mother than our mother had been. I asked her about this strange voice, and she told me that I should ignore such things.

"These are demons of ill omen," she said, for she had become a staunch puritan in her beliefs, influenced as she was by our father. "Do not go to those graves. Your brother is not sanctified."

Then she told me the story of how on the day my brother had died, our father buried him quickly in the middle of the night, embarrassed that the child had neither been baptized nor saved in any outward way. She had been five years old at the time, and she had asked our mother why she must not mention her dead brother again.

Our mother had told her, "God has taken him. Let God keep his secrets."

As Bathsheba explained it to me, there were demons and terrible spirits that lurked among the graves, and I should not wander there, nor seek solace at my twin's side. "The Lord Jesus wishes you to seek salvation only," she said. I was young enough to half believe her words, although I doubted that my brother was surrounded by demons, for if he were my twin, he slept with angels.

The voice, and these words, haunted me. Perhaps it was God, I thought, or just a voice that might arise in my head now and then. But I had the distinct impression that it was a voice I had never before heard, and, because I sat by the baby's grave, I attributed it to him.

The grave was one of several where the babies were buried, called in Welsh the Baban Claddfa, from the old days. It was on a hillside overlooking a slender river that ran for several miles.

I didn't know why the voice bade me carry it to the river.

I felt it was my brother, though how a baby dead many years would learn the English language and speak from heaven as a much older child, I had no notion.

I let this incident go by the wayside, although I mentioned it to my mother, who suggested that it might be the Virgin, despite the fact that it sounded like the voice of a boy very much my own age.

I doubt that I mentioned this to my father, who was a stern and unloving figure to me.

When, finally, vexed by the memory of this voice, I went one morning in the mud of spring to truly see for myself what this voice might've meant.

Chapter Two

A Mystery of Bones

1

I took my father's tools and dug the grave as if it were a rose needing to be replanted. I found the bundle a few feet down in the earth (for it was the custom, particularly in the rocky soil, to keep shallow graves on the hillsides, for graves were often moved to various locations, or else disinterred altogether and taken to a common grave after considerable time had passed). This was surely a morbid task for me to undertake, but I had spent too many nights wanting to see his bones, to see what I would have been, had I died so young, and to fulfill this request that I could not get free from in my mind.

When I opened the bundle, I saw what seemed to me the bones of a bird. His small, desiccated corpse—the darkened thin leather of skin stuck to bone. I cradled my twin in my arms and whispered to him that I hoped he was in heaven.

Then I carried the bundle to the river and sat down on the rocks, holding it. There was a shallow, quiet edge to the narrow river, rounded by stones placed there by the girls who came with their morning's washing. It was a bowl of still water, surrounded by the gently moving current around the stones. It was this that I would use for my baptismal font. I peered into the dark water and saw my reflection. How well I remember it, my small boy-face, the sadness in my eyes, and the sense that someone stood there with me, peering down at my reflection as well. I turned around quickly, but there was no one near me, or up on the hillside even.

I waited, wondering if his voice would come, but it did not.

It occurred to me that my brother had never been baptized. Perhaps this, I thought, was what the voice intended, the truth at the river I was meant to find.

So I leaned over and cupped my free hand in the water, and brought it up to the skull. I poured the icy water over it, saying things that sounded suitably biblical to me, a mix of words remembered from both the Catholic and Methodist services.

Again, I looked at my reflection, and felt as if there were something momentous about to happen, some faerie would come up from the water, perhaps, or God would offer a sign. But there was nothing. Just my face, wan and with that hungry look that poor boys have.

I held my brother's remains in my arms, cradling him the way our mother surely must have done.

And that is when I saw that the back edge of the skull had been crushed.

2

It wasn't a large hole that had been made in his skull, but fairly small, as if some tool had been used. The bone of the skull was cracked around it, and it was just big enough for me to press my finger into it.

Not knowing what to make of this, at least at that moment, I stared at it a while longer. I began to think about the Miasma that had come through when I'd been a baby, and imagined my brother Lloyd growing sicker soon after he was born. I had heard that surgeons sometimes did horrible things, and had seen a man who had a hole in his head from where a surgeon had to drill in order to relieve pressure. The man lived in our village and did not seem any worse for his cranial opening. Perhaps, I thought, my little brother had been sick, but the physician called to help might have tried some measure to relieve his pain or suffering. Perhaps. I didn't completely believe this, nor did I, then, want to find out the truth.

But it gnawed at me.

Thus, when I was ten years old, I discovered

how secrets are kept, and how they are often buried, yet refuse to remain underground.

3

My brother had been killed. Perhaps accidentally. But killed, nonetheless. By whom? I could guess, but I could not know for sure. Nor could I find out, because I would not know whom to trust with the question.

Someone had bashed his small head in, and then had not even had the decency to baptize him at the local church after death (which was sometimes done). Because, if he were baptized, a priest might notice the skull. It would be known that it was not the Miasma, but murder. I knew that my dead brother's message to me was about saving me from his murderer, and avenging his death. There was a monster in our house, and he was my father.

You may think it morbid of me, the little boy with the baby's bones in his hands, but I wrapped the bones carefully and hid them in a hollow of a tree. I covered over his grave, even going so far as to dig up patches of grass and press it into the muddy earth to make it seem as if it had not been disturbed. While I did this, I had the peculiar sense of being watched, but as was true at the river, no one seemed to be nearby.

At first, I kept my brother's bones in the tree for weeks, and then one night, I took them under my shirt and ragged coat and brought them home. I shared a room with my brothers, so it was not easy to hide anything in the house, but we had an outhouse in the back, shared with several other families. Behind the seat, there was an area where rags were kept. I laid the bones well under the rags, and checked on my brother regularly, speaking to the bones as if they could hear me, telling him what I was thinking and of my dreams and ambitions.

I went on this way, between work and school and home and the bones of my brother, for several years.

I held the conviction that my father, who was prone to violent outbursts and believed in the whipping post and the rod, was the murderer of my twin. I watched him carefully and avoided him when I could.

As time passed, my sister Bathsheba married a local boy who worked at the mill, and in the mornings, as a baker. My older brothers eventually began to seek their fortunes beyond the walls of our small home. I became, in the home, the eldest, and I clung to the uncomfortable safety of the room I shared with my younger brothers, nearly afraid of the future that awaited me, of a life of ash and coal, but also wanting to protect my brothers and sisters from my father's wrath. We clashed often, my father and I. More than once I had to shout at him for pummeling my younger siblings for some imagined sin or crime. As a result, I often took a beating myself in their stead.

Thoughts of Lloyd kept me up at night. Of the bones. Of the skull.

4

Victoria had been on the throne since I'd been six, and perhaps it was my rebellion against anything approaching propriety that got me to become a bit wild, compared to the other boys my age, who seemed beaten down by the mines and the ashy life we were forced to live.

I ran to pleasure whenever I could, whether it was candy or clotted cream or the bodies of the local girls. I truly loved pleasure, and as I got older, the pleasures became more enticing.

I lost my physical virginity at sixteen to a factory girl in Newcastle, whose thighs seemed so big around that I got lost inside her for minutes at a time.

Chapter Three

The Rite of Manhood

1

She smothered me with her affections and her affectations, no doubt expecting marriage and a life away from the sooty skies and endless hours of working in a dark coal basement by the light of sulfur, her lungs growing blacker and her heart growing weary, even in her early twenties. She was pretty, for a poor young woman, as I was perhaps handsome for a poor youth, and we found our pleasure by meeting in the woods and sheep meadows behind the shambling manor houses on the hillside. It was a dangerous meeting. Many a boy had an ear cut off for wandering on the landowner's property. Still, it was early spring and the master of the house was off in distant London. The youth of the area often dallied there, finding the warmth of lust in the tall grasses, or against a rock, or behind the old stone wall overlooking the paddock. I recall now that she swore like a boatswain in a brothel when I brought my greater self into her, and she clutched me around the middle and whispered obscenities that would've made a whore blush.

This was my first rite of manhood, the chief pleasure of one who worked from four in the morning until eight at night from the age of eight years onward. It was the only happy moment of my life at home. Pleasure, physical pleasure, taught me that there was more to the world than what I had known. The stroking, the rocking, the gentle tug of war between her skin and mine, the lapping of tongues and the wet feeling between us, and within my own body, the building of pressure into an explosion . . . it is not a subject that the world speaks much of, but for those of us who are born to want, it is the first we know that within our own beings, we can create our own worlds. The flesh itself provides knowledge, entertainment, craft, and heaven.

Pleasure led me to pleasure.

My next chief pleasure became learning.

I learned about physical pleasure then, but books were more my calling. I taught myself to read by quizzing the local schoolmistress, and eventually seducing her as well. She was not more than two years my senior, and we had bouts of pleasure in bed, on the floor, against the schoolroom wall. She taught me what I had not been able to learn in many years of our one-room schoolhouse. She brought me great books and

Latin primers. She met my thrusts with declarations taken from Shakespeare and Marlowe. We sweated against each other, making ungodly noises that would surely make the angels weep, as I made her read me *Paradise Lost*. This was my earliest blasphemy, for we moved on to the original Italian of Dante's *Inferno*, and I was never not inside her body as she taught me that foreign tongue with her own tongue.

My love of England grew as she cupped me in her hands and whispered sonnets and lusty ballads of medieval origin in my ear.

2

In the meantime, I managed to work the mines fewer hours, and instead took on shoemaking and clock-fixing work, as I was fairly mechanically inclined. I found a burning within me to learn more, do more, make more money, and find more pleasure. I found pleasure in things outside the bedroom, in whatever new that I could learn, whatever theory I could grasp. I borrowed books on physics and naturalism from the manor's library, whose master had begun to enjoy my company as I repaired his mistress's boot, or worked on the great clock in his grand hall.

My sexual companion, whom I shall, for discretion's sake, call Miss French or Bootsy, as I called her for the peculiarly tromping but elegant lady's boot she wore, didn't like my other work.

She felt that I should be available to her for her pleasure and to assuage her never-quenched loneliness.

Eventually, we tired of each other, for I had learned more from her than she had from me. And the scandal came out—from her own mouth, for she could not refrain from boasting to her sewing circle that she regularly trapped the most handsome youth in our little village and intended to marry him once she was with child. These were not enlightened times, and although every schoolboy knew of the factory girls and their easy ways, we had fire and brimstone on Sundays and were taught that our lower regions were tools of Satan, who longed to misguide us and condemn us to eternal perdition.

It was a horrifying moment for me, to walk into our hovel and have my mother slap me for "that devilry," and for my father to want to throw me bodily from the house. In some families, fathers might be proud of their son's swordsmanship, but my father was puritanical and harsh to each of us, and believed we were the stain of sin for his having married someone not Methodist but "of the Roman scourge," as he called the Catholic Church. We children were mongrels, unworthy of salvation, unworthy of anything but lifelong penitence.

My father and I began fighting, arguing, throwing chairs—of which we had few to spare—and cursing at each other. My mother sat in the corner and wept as my father chastised me for my ways, and I crowed about wanting to leave this graveyard of a home. Finally, I drew out my trump card.

The bones themselves would speak.

3

I dashed through the back window and ran to the outhouse. Digging through the rags, I picked up the bundle of my brother's bones and sped straightaway back into the house, like a monkey leaping tree to tree. I held the small sack up, crowing, "I know what happened to Lloyd!"

My father put his hands on his hips, eyeing me with suspicion. "What are you yapping about?"

"What you did! What you did to him! My brother. My twin brother. I know it wasn't the Miasma!" With this I opened the sack, and poured my brother out onto the hearthstone, near my mother, who screamed when she saw it. Although I had some remorse for this overly dramatic revelation, I felt it was the moment that needed to happen. The truth had to come out! I had to throw in their faces what I had known and kept secret for several years.

"And what is it you think you know, you worthless whelp?" His voice had quieted a bit, but was like an incision in a fresh wound: sharp and painful and precise. "What is it you think you've discovered?"

"Dear God!" my mother cried out, all of a sudden. "He died of the Miasma. It was terrible. Dear God in heaven!" Her sobs were now peppered with little shrieks of agony, the like of which I had never before heard from anyone.

"No," I said, feeling triumphant to finally bring this to light. "He didn't. You knew it." I pointed at my father as a judge to the convicted. "You killed him. You bashed his head in. You murdered my brother! You didn't even have the decency to baptize him! You buried him in secret, in the night! You monster!"

My father shook his head, glaring at me all the while. "You fool," he spat. "Is this how you repay your mother for caring for you, for cleaning you, for feeding you? Is this how you repay us for giving you food and shelter and a Christian upbringing?"

"You're a monster!" I shouted at him, pointing my finger as if laying a curse.

"Look at you," he said. "Look at you, grave-digging, stirring things up, lifting the skirts of the local whores and ruining girls, generating bastards for all we know. You, my boy, are the monster."

My mother's weeping increased, and she covered her face with her hands. Through her heaving sobs, I heard her say the Hail Mary.

Monstrously, my father began laughing, roaring loud. "You want to know what happened to your twin? You want to know why he is in that grave and you are not?" Turning to my mother, he said, "Why don't you tell him, my love? Why don't you let your son know why he is alive and his twin lies in the graves of the angels?"

I looked at my mother, but her face was covered and her weeping copious. I was torturing her with this, I felt. I had not wanted to reach this position of uncorking the family vintage, of raising my brother's death and its mystery, but I had done so, nonetheless. Her heartache was readily apparent, and I realized I was the curse of the household.

I did not belong there anymore.

What surprised me the most in all this was that my father did not raise his hand against me. I almost had the feeling he was frightened of me now.

I went to embrace my mother, but her trembling body seemed unwelcoming. I gathered my brother's bones, as many as I could quickly grab, including his skull and ribcage, and put them in the sack.

My father had calmed, although his eyes smoldered as he watched me.

"I am leaving. For good," I said.

My father bid me good riddance, saying I was far too old to be sharing their roof anyway, that my older brothers had left at fourteen and I should have followed their examples and that I had brought heartache and damnation into his home.

I left, with my mother's sobs like a banshee's wail, following me along the streets of the village.

I thought of Lloyd, the small bones in the sack

bundle and the chips of his gentle barely formed skull pushed in, smashed. I felt confused by my father's taunting, but my mother's tears had been unequivocal. That my father had killed him seemed certain. Or did it? Had my mother, perhaps, murdered him? Why had my father laughed at mention of his death? My mind conjured possibilities: that my mother, with two babies still nursing, and now twins, had not enough milk to go around. Or perhaps she had been sick after our births and had dropped my brother, or again, the thought that a surgeon had been called to relieve some pressure on his brain. Why had my father laughed? What monster would laugh when remembering the death of his child?

I had no answers still.

Whatever had happened to my brother would remain a mystery, for I would abandon the family of my birth and seek my fortune in the world.

Chapter Four

A New Life

1

I had nothing and no one. Even my school-mistress would not take me, for I was now not good enough for the likes of her, though she had been painted with the Whore of Babylon's powder brush. At midnight, I banged on the door of the baker's shop, over which my sister Bathsheba, her husband, and my niece slept. Bathsheba came out eventually and told me that Jesus would guide me, that I needed to give my soul over to the Lord and to repent of my sins.

"You do not know what you do now," she said. "You believe you understand the world and its forces, but you have followed the ways of the flesh. You must repent, and look to the word of God. Forsake this carnal pastime, and make a scourge of your flesh." She had recited my father's words so much that they were her normal way of speaking.

"You are the godforsaken," I told her, and left her there, in the dark of her doorway with these final words, "You will come to know the devil yourself one day, and your Lord will not pluck you from his fiery arms."

I was nearly eighteen, and without a place to sleep.

2

That night I slept on the high summer grass, and stared up at the stars, or what could be seen of them. Even at night, the black smoke roiled in the heavens.

I spoke aloud to God, unsure if my youthful nature would keep him deaf to my pleas.

But I had an answer by morning, as to my question of what I should do next.

The railroad industry was growing rapidly and had been since my birth. The news of railway races, testing their speed and comfort, came to us weekly from Liverpool and Manchester. The plans of expanding the rails to all parts of the British Isles filled my dreams with exploration. On the continent, great changes occurred as well, and it all made me believe that we were entering a new phase of human existence, when there was nothing that could not be touched, seen, experienced. I wanted to be part of it. The industry around the rails was about to grow, and there were jobs to the north and east. Industries must advance, and I knew that I had talents with numbers and an engineering sense, as well as my newfound knowledge of literature and the past, which could be applied to this new world within the old world that would mean something important for me. We were entering more fully the Age of Machines, and I knew it was my opportunity to build a fortune.

At the mines in Newcastle, we'd had railway-like trams for mining. I had repaired them at times, and knew many aspects of their engineering that even the older men did not know. I knew I could somehow make my way in the world with the newer, more modern railways that would carry passengers long distances. I had an uncle in Manchester, so I'd been told, though I had never met him. I would somehow get there, sleep in his shed, and work in some capacity. I was good with numbers, and now had a decent education in English, with a smattering of Latin and Italian. Surely, I could find better work than shoveling coal or shearing sheep.

So I set off, walking, hitching rides with the less reputable carriage lines, sleeping beneath bridges, feeling, as one does at that age, the freedom of life. The freedom from family. The sense that the world is about to open up for you as you discover it.

The belief that it is a benevolent dictator, this life.

3

So I left all I had known, begged, borrowed, and stole my way to my uncle's. When passing through a large enough town, and having no money to speak of, I went to the local Anglican church, which would have a comfortable chapel. I would go in and sleep on the pews until such a time in the morning I would be thrown out. In one such town, I was thrown from the premises early, and went to sleep among the graves. I brought out my brother's bones, and, finding a fresh grave that had not yet been filled with its tenant, buried my brother at the bottom of the newly dug plot and covered this over with sod.

Lloyd had a Christian burial at last, at least in terms of location. Both my father and mother would think this a blasphemy, as they each believed the Anglicans were the most corrupt of all the heathen churches.

I slept well, atop the grave of a former magistrate of the town, and when I awoke, the local priest found me there and offered me a fine breakfast and three pounds from the poor box to help me on my way to my uncle's home.

4

My uncle lived in the heart of Manchester, an industrial town that was growing and full of possibilities. Although others might call it dirty and boring, I found the streets of Manchester to be like the firmament itself: It was wall-to-wall possibility, and sometimes, that is all a young man with less than a penny in his pocket and a talent for fixing things needs.

Uncle Meyrick was now called Maurice, had taken the last name Gravesend, as was the fashion then (to modify a name that sounded too old-fashioned or perhaps even of a lower caste; it was becoming the norm to Anglify it as completely as possible). So I too became, not Iestyn ap Graver, but Justin Gravesend, and with the name adjustment, felt as if a whole new life were offered, with a whole new teat from which to suck.

Uncle Maurice lived in a hulking cottage made up of two rooms, with a kitchen in a separate small house outside. He welcomed me like the prodigal son. He had a heart as big as the city itself, and I knew my luck had changed when we met and he embraced me as if he had been waiting his whole life to see one of his nephews. He made some choice words about my father and mother, and then told me to go and bathe and he would buy me some new clothes for my new life.

When I had shaven and sponged myself in an ill-fitting tub, he returned with clothes that, to me, seemed spun from gold, yet they were ordinary work clothes of the time.

Uncle Maurice was a jovial drunk with a wide pink face and an excellent way about him that made few women love him but many men adore his company. He was a raconteur who enjoyed brandy and cigars, and had learned to cheat at cards without offending his partners. He made his living by running a tobacco and sundries shop near the waterfront. He lived partly off this, and partly from a yearly allowance from the estate of his great-grandfather, from which my family had been disinherited. He was generous to a fault, and I grew to love him as my own father.

He introduced me to men at the rail yard, who tested me for keeping books for the railway. Soon I was earning my keep and contributing to my uncle's household. I even managed to send a little money each month to my mother. I had become worried about her cough (of which she'd written me) and that she might put some savings aside for her old age.

Now and then, my sister Bathsheba would write to me and tell me how badly I'd treated our father and how God wished for me to return to Him so that I might understand my sinful ways. I ignored her letters and would send her brief notes telling her that I was happy to hear about her latest child, my new nephew or niece, and I included a few pennies for the child's upkeep. I held no animosity toward her, for I considered Bathsheba a lost soul in that horrible village, stuck in a life I had so gladly escaped. My other brothers and sisters fared better and got far away, some of them even going to America, others, to jobs in the Midlands, where new industries were just being born.

I enjoyed these several months, but before I was nineteen, Uncle Maurice warned me that I shan't want to be adding numbers in a ledger book my whole life. "You need more than this, Just, you have a mind that's better than your beginnings."

He meant for me to enter the university, and so I submitted to the barrage of tests and entrance examinations, primarily oral, to attend. I failed some of them, but impressed the faculty enough that I was allowed two courses of study to begin. I had a talent with biology, particularly regarding human anatomy, which I could only attribute to my many hours gazing at my brother's bones. So I was to study the natural world with seminars in anatomy and physiology and literature, although I would not end up as either a surgeon or professor, two vocations that seemed to require a wealthy family in order to rise within the ranks.

Within weeks, I had added more studies. I attended class in the mornings and worked the ledger books at night. My new classes included botany and biology, as well as astronomy, when time permitted. I began reading the new books then being published: the works of the American Nathaniel Hawthorne, Charles Dickens's *The Personal History of David Copperfield*, and Alfred Lord Tennyson's *In Memoriam*, which affected me greatly. It was a world that was so different from the blackened skies of my childhood that I felt at times like I had died and gone to heaven. I found I had a genuine hunger for learning, as if it had been an essential nutrient deprived me, and I found there was more to learn than my ardent schoolmistress had even suspected.

Despite the roiling of the world's events, news from America and the Continent of upheavals, and even the news from London, I hid from the world, into the literature I could find. The languages I could learn. Pages I turned until my fingers nearly bled, and my eyes blurred. I ignored the physical and grew a bit fat around the belly, but soon learned to fast and keep from gaining the odd stone or two by restricting my diet nearly to a prisoner's fare. I added boxing to my repertoire of exercise, as well as a popular athletic game called rugby that I'd been taught by the rich boys at my college who seemed to spend most of their days in lackadaisical pursuits and narcissistic rituals. I admired them, to some extent, for their inability or interest in making money. They had no need of it, for they were the sons of estates and landowners and they were at university merely to pass the time before they'd return to the manor houses of their boyhood and work the tenants to their deaths. They spoke of war as if it were an extension of their favorite sports, and they had no fear of the future. Nor did they have a sense that it held possibilities. In this, I felt bad for them. Additionally, I felt a bit of grief when they spoke of our college, for they were the low end of their schools—their fellows and siblings had gone on to better universities, while they were stuck in Manchester, not quite bright enough to make it to Oxford. I, myself, felt that Manchester was the peak of the kind of education I could get, and it had more to offer than I believe these fellows knew.

While there, I read every piece of literature, learned Latin and French and German and Russian. I studied politics and the law. I found myself with nosebleeds from staying up all night several days in a row in order to keep working and keep studying. I was motivated by a sheer desire to never return to the factories and the coal pits and the farmlands and stink of sheep and the taste of two-day-old kidney pie or cold porridge or mutton stew left too long in the pot.

I wanted a finer life, and so I avoided more entanglements of the flesh, sure that some comely but desperate lass would pull down her underthings and press herself onto me in order to saddle me with children and a bleak future. I had seen it happen often enough to other boys from the colliery.

I wanted to be as far away from the black skies of my childhood as possible, and away from the father who threw me against walls to keep me silent and the mother who thought I would go to hell if I spoke one word against my father, as if he were Jesus Christ himself. I knew that there were people with money, the men who owned the mines, who owned the lands, whose sons went to Eton and Harrow and Darlington Rows, schools where the skies were clean and no one sickened from daily living. Those boys would go on to Oxford and Cambridge and the world's universities, or were beside me at Manchester, while I, and my kind, would enter the dark mines and bring up the coal to heat the rich men's homes.

I wanted to live their lives, and stay far from the one in which I had been dumped, like ash in a bin.

And so I finished my studies early, having been one of the most brazen and unstoppable of students, driven to master language and history and oratory, and become more than a keeper of figures and numbers, and move into the realm of which the rich boys I knew had no regard simply because it meant nothing to them: I wanted to be a master of the world.

5

When I was twenty-one, I lost my spiritual virginity. I met a man I shall call the Necromancer, who took me by the hand and led me down pathways into the human and eternal mind, and introduced me to the mystical union of those who influence the Earth, the Planets, and the Cosmos.

And he taught me about Magick for the first time.

Visionary 2

My manhood grows long and fat and begins to speak from its narrow mouth, and tells of the pain that is inflicted upon it when it is used to bring forth life. Then I see it is merely my phallus again, engorged, and I find the one who offers a portal for me, a doorway to enter and then seal the entrance again, my sacrifice who has ingested the herb and whose glassy eyes turn toward me, lips parted slightly, between a gasp and a prayer and love.

I press myself there, feel the dry warmth, and I call the names of my kindred, my brethren, to bear witness to the lightning that I shall bring into myself, into the tomb where we meet, through the altar of the one who has offered to me the most sacred vessel.

The jackals of that other realm begin to howl for their meat, which still writhes in my arms as I beat myself into that world, the very geometry of my flesh expanding outward, as it webs and stretches, reaching like a mollusk's foot to touch the sandy bottom of some new sea.

Chapter Five

London Adventure

1

During the spring after my twenty-first birthday, some of the rich young students, who had so recently seemed like boys to me but were now gentlemen, invited me to go with them down to London. These were young men who had paid no attention to me in the early years of my study, for I was poor and spoke as a poor man and dressed as a poor man. I was from the rustic gutter, in their opinion, and no matter how well I learned the finer turns of phrases, no matter how well my uncle's old clothes fit me, and no matter that my income from working the accounting books on the rails in the city put pound notes in my pocket, I was somehow lesser.

There was no way around this issue of class. It continues on today, but in my youth, it was at its worst.

The boys who were only just becoming men

sneered and strutted, and yet were great fun in their own ways. But they never let me forget my station, and when I saw their servants, who often brought them tea in the common rooms of the university, I realized that my status in life might even be beneath their butlers and maids. And yet, through my limited wit and basic intelligence and no doubt their own natural curiosity about a rustic who got top marks, these rich boys gradually warmed to me, and eventually, two of them spent more and more time with me at the local ale-house, which was slumming for them.

"You're a jolly fellow," one said to me one evening, downing a pint. "You aren't like the others."

"No, you're not," his chum said. "I suppose it's not true what they say about colliers and their brains—being blackened with soot."

This passed for wit, and, wanting to get along, I laughed with them, then drank with them, and eventually awoke on the floor of their rooms, feeling as if I, too, were a gentleman. Or, at the very least, passing for one. I was vain and foolish, of course, but I was young and wanting a better life. Their acceptance meant the world to me.

One of my new friends said something that I couldn't possibly understand at the time, but which seemed important. I heard him in the next room say to his friend, "It's hard to believe it's this one."

"True," the other said. "But I was there. I heard it said."

At the time, this just seemed like idle conversation between them, and I didn't make anything of it.

2

It is pathetic to think this now, but at the time, I wanted to be part of that larger world, the one that would put me as far away from the coal mines as possible. And I felt that I was moving in that direction. With these newfound friends, perhaps I would get there.

3

It was April, and I'd been studying too hard, poring over Latin texts and trying to decipher the medical books I'd just found that dealt with aspects of the human body. Learning about the physical body was the most discouraging part of my education, and after doing so I wished I had remained ignorant, and happy.

I found myself drawn to medicine, perhaps not as practice, but as an area of serious study. I gained access, through professors who believed I would be a credit to them, to the great arenas of the medical school.

I watched as corpses were opened and revealed. It soured my stomach to the smells of the human body, dead or alive, and, fascinated though I was by the human reproductive organs, I did not enjoy seeing them under the carving knife of the local physician whom I passed daily on the streets.

Watching the scientific evisceration of the human corpse made me wonder if all human life was not just some burp of existence with nothing to redeem it. After all, where was God for the body at the center of the room? That man or woman had not risen from the dead to ascend into heaven.

That corpse was just meat on a table, to be flayed and filleted and cut into morsels for the surgeons in attendance, and the curious students, such as myself. It was a butcher shop of humanity, and I could not see in the scissors and saws of the professors of medicine, whose aprons were brown from the blood of countless operations, whose instruments were thick with the congealed blood and bits of hair of the many who had died beneath their learned care, God—anywhere. God or Christ or the Virgin. Merely the utter waste and futility of all human endeavor.

This is what we come to, I thought. My youthful dreams of glory and wealth were nothing, because they would not prolong my life, they would not reduce misery, they would not turn the tide of the greatest problem of all human existence, which is that the only Queen of Heaven (or hell or earth) is Mother Death, Mater Mort, Persephone in her matronly aspect, gobbling pomegranate seeds while she raises her fingernails to slice at the hearts of humankind, throwing back her head to laugh at all human ambition and desire.

Even Uncle Maurice and his young wife (whom he'd just met and married the previous winter) recognized my newfound despondency and perhaps a morbid turn of mind from all the hours of study and examination. Uncle Maurice felt I needed an interlude before my final few courses were complete. "You're a young man. Being young doesn't last forever. Go enjoy April. Meet some fine women. Drink, rest, see the world a bit," he told me. How he could possibly have come from the same family that had produced my father, I still, to this day, can't fathom. He was the most generous soul, and loving. He was a man among men, happy with his lot, constant in his affection, and never felt that the world was anything but a wonderful place.

I had avoided the pleasures of life in favor of the pleasures of the brain, which I found could have no equal, so I thought, in human relations. But I took the advice, even accepting a few quid from my uncle, and managed to get, through my employer, free fares for my two school chums on the rails that would take us to the great city, which I had not yet seen. I had learned that very rich young men expected to be given things for free.

"Prepare to be humbled," Wendy, short for Wendell, the older of the two told me, crushing a ten-pound note into my hand, which seemed like a fortune, as the train slowly entered the city proper. "Now run and get us some libation from the platform, will you? I have an enormous thirst."

We drank much, laughed much, slept, and nearly missed a connection at one point. We ate too many watercress-and-butter sandwiches at a small station buttery when we had a two-hour delay between trains.

It was our fourth train on the voyage. In between trains, we had to catch hansoms to make our connection. I was weary and bleary-eyed, and ready to just sleep when he said, "This is London. This is the place for all-hours debauchery."

Always an avid sport for debauchery, or so I thought, I imagined beautiful women, magnificent clubs, and smart men with brilliant ideas. I regained my energies and felt renewed as we entered the station.

My first sight of the city had confirmed what I'd read of it in books: It was the center of the growing empire, and seemed to me like Rome in its ancient glory.

But like Rome, it had its filth and squalor.

4

When we left the train, and went to find a hansom, I saw nothing but a cesspool. The train station itself was fashionably kept, but just beyond it began what seemed a human swamp of misery and carelessness, its stench like the terrible river. The sky was not clear, but had become nearly as blackened as the sky of my home. It was a city of greatness and despair, like twins holding hands.

One dead, one living; one failing, one advancing. I did not like it at all, and had to be convinced by my companions that there was more to this New Rome than met the eye.

Once further into town, the beauty of it came about again, the palaces and grand apartments, the boulevards and parks, all of which I'd studied. Apartments that seemed like palaces lined the beautiful boulevards, great white buildings and skies above that faded from black to pale blue. It was as if we'd stepped from a museum gallery in which all the paintings were of lepers, into one in which the pantheon of Greek gods suddenly appeared. My companions pointed out the fashionable clubs, the houses of great ladies and gentlemen—many I knew from reading the newspapers, but none of whom seemed human to me, for they were beyond the rabble of mankind I had known all my life. Statesmen and great novelists and war heroes and legendary actors—all living within several blocks of one another, in this mansion of a city that we toured as we went up to my friend's London home.

But I could not shake those first things I'd seen outside the train station. They put the poverty that hovered in parts of Manchester to shame. They put the hopelessness of Cwthshire and its ash heaps to shame, as well. That this grand whore of a city could have festering syphilitic wounds like this, that on her painted face, a gilded beauty, and her gown was the finest silk, but still tinged with mud at the ragged hem, and beneath her great skirts, dirty underclothes, and fistulas in her private parts from decay and disease.

And yet James and Wendy brought me to a fine townhouse opposite the Regent's Park, where the sound of carriages arriving, the shiny horses that seemed to have finer lives than the poor of the city, and the laughter of fine young ladies seemed worlds away from the filthy undergarments from which we'd entered. The place was full of servants, some of whom were there to draw the bath, to dress us, to bring us drink, to coddle us in every way that a man is not meant to be coddled. Curiously, the servants were all beautiful, both the women and the men. The men were young and strong with the features of gods, and the women were of heart-shaped face and large bosom, and seemed like beautiful statues brought to life to do the bidding of the rich. It was as if the rich only hired the cream of the crop in terms of looks, breeding, and character. Or so I thought at the moment I was introduced to the employees of the house. One particular maid caught my eye— she was a slip of a girl of nineteen, but looked as if she could've been the subject of a great painter, like Vermeer. A young manservant had a face as white as dove's wings, and spoke a better class of the English language than even I could muster. I felt I should serve both of them tea and shine their shoes, for these servants were truly my betters.

No wonder my school chums had seemed so soft and tender—they had nothing to do other than explore pleasure and mischief and whatever they could dream up. They had no reason not to do as they pleased. I envied them, and yet felt bad that they had not ever done anything by and for themselves. It was as if, despite their youth and minds and athletic abilities, they were helpless babies in the crib.

And yet there was immense beauty and possibility in their world, as well. To be bathed by a maidservant pouring warm water down your back, while a manservant scrubbed your feet—that was as if I had died and gone to heaven—but to add to this, a beautiful young lady at the harp, just beyond the bath, playing soothing dulcet tones on those strings had me wishing that I'd been born to this life rather than to the other one, of struggle and harsh words.

I am sad to say that I soon forgot that darker part of London, and instead, like my companions, bathed and made ready for a night on the town. I could easily take on the life of a fop, if given half the chance.

5

Drunk by six, having Madeira and something they called "malmsey," I wobbled and laughed too easily and seemed far, far too joyous and excited—"Like a farm boy!" James slapped me on the back, having emerged from his bath half-naked and dripping on the floors of his great-aunt Minnie's house, a pure white confection that might've been a wedding cake. He told me briefly of the house's history. The place was bought from a dissolute rich French cleric named Alphonse Constant, and thus was called "Constant House" by James's family, who renovated it within the past decade. He looked at me as if he realized his family history lesson was a bit of a bore. "You drink much more and you shall be sick."

"I shan't be sick, because I am too well," I said, not certain of my own logic.

"We are due at dinner at half past," James commanded, rapping on the door for Wendy, who had napped. He turned back to me, a broad smile on his face. "You've never met society ladies, have you?"

"Not that I'm aware," I said.

"Well, the protocol is set. Wen and I are the third-tier suitors in their world, and they are a class above us in many ways." He said this all with a serious air.

"There is actually a class above you?"

He snorted with laughter. "They think so. They have more money and better blood. But we have charm. We entertain them, allow them to charm us, we charm them, and then afterward all the men go to the drawing room or, in this case, the library, for important talk."

"Sounds dreadful."

248

"It can be. But it's necessary for the evening's entertainment. Say, you'll need to dress better for these ladies." He went through the giant wardrobe in the room that he claimed had been his since childhood. He began throwing shirts and shoes and trousers all around the floor. I watched his disregard for the fabrics, for the exquisitely tailored clothes and nearly wept.

"Whatever's the matter, old boy? Why so glum?"

"I . . . I just think they're beautiful. And too good for me."

"Clothes? These clothes? These are nearly ready for the rubbish heap," he said.

But I had never seen such fine clothing in my life, all in one wardrobe.

"Your Aunt Minnie won't like all this mess," I said, chiding him.

"Minnie lives here by my good graces. She has an allowance that comes from my father's estate, and if she isn't good to me, she is out on her bum. She knows this is my home first, hers second," he said it all breezily, as if the welfare of his great-aunt were simply a whim. Going through all the stiff white shirts and hanging collars, he drew one out and threw it to me. "That about should fit you, and here," he said, a pair of dark trousers sailing my way, landing on my head. "If those don't quite fit, we can pinch them in with a hatpin or something."

I dove into the clothes, and felt every inch a

rich gentleman just holding them in my hands. Two servants were called in to help me dress, which, for better or worse, aroused my "sleeping soldier," as James called it. But this was the strangest sensation of pleasure I'd ever experienced: to be touched simply while being dressed, as if I needed a staff of two to make sure all buttonhooks were fastened, cuffs and collar in place. It excited me just to feel that power over someone else. And I felt guilty, as well, for this way of living seemed wrong. I imagined my mother and father in their home, patching together clothes, sewing into the night, taking charity from the church to make sure they had enough blankets in the winter. Yet, I suppose, being a young man, and prone to pleasure and idleness, I was able to dismiss my guilt and my thoughts of my own beginnings. I was in a different milieu now.

James offered me quick lessons in etiquette: the knives, the forks, the way to eat peas, the way to slice the meat, and then added, "You'll meet several eligible young girls. You are not to mention snooker, only billiards. Nothing of rugby—too uncouth. You must not talk of Manchester, for it will bore them. Instead . . ." he paused, conjuring a thought. "Well, see here, Justy, they want to be wooed. Listen to their gossip. Nod your head when they feel they have a point to make about which neighborhood has become less fashionable. They'll adore you, I daresay. Do not give in to the temptation to make love to them. They will consider you beneath them. They are looking for suitable catches. You are not one for them—now, don't be hurt. You don't want these girls. None of them are pretty in the least. They're rather plain, in fact. Plain but rich."

"Don't you find this charade despicable?"

He raised an eyebrow, considering. "Not in the least. I was raised for this, just as you," he swatted me lightly on the nose. "Well, just as you don't find the life of a collier despicable. It's just how we live."

"Then why dine with them?" I asked. "Why go through with this?"

"I intend to marry one of them," he said. "Her name is Anya. Her father is first cousin to the Czar, and her mother is one of the Greys, one of the old fashionable families of London. She is richer than I shall ever be. She is young now. Too young. But when she is of a more reasonable age, with girlish foolishness behind her, I will ask for her hand and be given it. She has an allowance that can keep us enjoying our holdings for both of our lives. And her breasts are like melons." He saw my slightly lost look. "Don't look at me like that, mate." He said the word "mate" with a tincture of venom, and it was his way of making fun of my background. It stung. I'd heard it before from the other students who came from money. They were slumming to be in college with those of us who were out of our class. They never let us forget it. "She's pleasant," he continued, "and I very much enjoy being with her. But I don't worry that it's that kind of love that the poets go on about. It's breeding, Justy. She's a virginal heiress with little world experience. She was raised to marry someone like me, and I have spent considerable time ensuring that she will be mine. We're different from you and your people. You have liberties in your daily life, but men like Wendy and I, we have to think about our families and our traditions. There's more to life than just love and chance. There's my great-aunt Minnie to think of, and I support my brother's wife, since he abandoned her. And my father's business needs building. Marriage is not about that passion idea. It's a union that serves the empire, and creates wealth and supports the lower classes as well." He said this all with rehearsed conviction, the way one might overhear someone in church reciting the Nicene Creed.

"Ah," I said, refusing to argue with my jolly companion. "Perhaps I should not drink so much. It may lead me to believe as you."

"Socrates said that bad men live that they may eat and drink, whereas good men eat and drink that they may live. Therefore, we must be good men, for we shall eat and drink to live tonight. But do not worry," he said, coming over to put his hands on my shoulders. He looked at me quite seriously. "We'll abandon the old men and the virgins and go see the whores after dinner."

Chapter Six

How the Rich Eat

1

Dinner was as I expected. The food was a delight: lobster bisque, truffles with pudding, a delicious roast beef and mutton, and fruits of such exotic variety that I thought it had been shipped from Araby.

The wines poured, the brandies sparkled, and I felt fat as a Christmas goose by the end of the meal, and pained from it. The dinner guests were the cause of any indigestion. I spent a stuffy, smothering three hours in which old women spoke of Tennyson and Elizabeth Barrett as if they were radicals, spoke of America as if it would soon become a colony again, and seemed to believe that it was the fashion to flirt in the most obvious ways with much younger men. Most of the young women talked of the latest fashion and musicians and the actors of the London stage. They bored me more than their elders. James's young lady, Anya, was different.

2

She sat across the table from me, and at first I didn't glance her way. But when I did, it was her voice that first captured me: an elegant, modulated voice that was not in her head or nasal region, as the other young women's, but deep in her throat, indicating a knowledge of her own body and a certain confidence and serious nature. When I saw her, I held my breath but a moment. An angel of delicacy and purity. She had the porcelain skin so admired in the day, but her cheeks were flushed and red, and she had a bit of sun around her nose and eyes, which I found utterly charming. This was one who did not avoid the noonday sun, nor did she hide from a task. She had the kind of figure in which young men delight, and auburn tresses that fell in what could only be called ringlets around her face, to her shoulders, not pulled back and tightened with ribbons as the others her age had done. Something about her reminded me of my puritanical sister, Bathsheba, who had been a more rustic beauty, but of similar charms. Perhaps it was my sense of purity, of them both. Of the angel. Of the saint. And yet somewhere lurking beneath the skin, there was the whiff of sensuality, if not decadence (yes, I had felt this even with my sister

Bathsheba, and often wondered if she had turned to the local church and hellfire and brimstone because she had felt so drawn to the very pleasures for which she had chastised me).

Beyond the pleasure of sight and sound, Anya had a nearly aggressive wit, and a direct way of speaking that seemed utterly foreign at the table. Contrary to how James had described her (including his not knowing her precise age), she was an intensely intelligent girl of eighteen, who wanted to discuss world politics while her companions offered up bored looks. She was attractive to the eye, and very much the image, to me, of temperate beauty. Her money meant nothing to me, but as I listened to her and watched her as she spoke, I realized that she was a woman to whom I could attach my affections. And I felt it—sitting at the table— the biological growl. As I looked at her, she ignited that animal passion inside me. It wasn't the shape of her breasts or the softness of her powdered skin that made me want her. It was her way of speaking, her interest in France and Germany, in the changes in Mexico, and the news of the abolitionists in America. She was an aware, awake mind, and were she not too young for my interests, I would have, perhaps, invited her for a walk that night to discuss literature and foreign governments. My interest in Anya carried me through the dinner, surrounded by the other dreadful women and men.

The men were not much better, and in some cases, less so, for they spoke of very little except to comment on matters of empire and honor. There was an admiral of the Queen's Navy, and a Scot who was Lord Something of Something, and a young man who was acclaimed as a fine musician who said not a word all night beyond "Please," and "Thank you." James and Wendy were in rare form, pouring libations when the servants hadn't come around fast enough, and chattering with the women, asking the admiral about wars and campaigns and the sea, and generally fitting in perfectly. I definitely felt that they were out of place at university. It was a bauble for them, or a small medal to add to a collection that they'd keep in a small wooden box on their dressing tables for the rest of their lives. They belonged not among scholars, but in this milieu, as much as did the wall hangings and the pretty birds in their cages in the conservatory. I began to see their money as the doors of a gaol, shutting them in, keeping them safe and away from life itself.

Because I'd buried myself in books and work, I had not been around so many people who were idle in all my life. The phrase kept coming to me, that the devil makes work for idle hands. The devil's work intrigued me.

I was quizzed from all quarters about the quaint life in a colliery, of what it was like to birth a sheep, although I could not go into much detail for risk of offending one of these silly girls. They treated me as a freak in a show, and in some ways they seemed surprised that a dirty ignorant boy from a distant village, a mongrel in their eyes, could clean up so well, become educated to a moderate degree, and even have friends like James and Wendell. The most annoying questions had to do with my future employment, for as I responded with my plans and interests, I could tell that they thought it such a novelty to have someone at table who actually had worked in any capacity and would continue to work. There is probably nothing on earth worse than a class snob from London, and I felt every ounce of the condescension in the room, like it was a lightning bolt that hit me, again and again.

3

At one point, toward the end of dinner, I had to go use the privy (as we often called the outhouse when I had been a boy). In the great mansion in which we had our dinner, there were two possibilities for this. In the back alley, behind the house, there was an actual outhouse, made from brick and stone rather than the thrown-together wood of my childhood. But upstairs, there was a room off the bath for this. I chose this latter method of pissing away the wine I'd been drinking, mainly because I wanted to see this elaborate room.

As I went into the bath area, and through it to get to what the owners of the house called a closet, the door was partially open, and I heard someone already using the facility.

I stood outside the little room, but from the slightly open door, I caught a glimpse of the one who used it. It was Anya. I saw a bit of her neck and the curve of her breast. I felt terrible low-class for looking, but I decided to move closer. I had never seen a lady in this position, and if you think me a worm for doing so, so be it. I went to the edge of the doorframe and observed her. She sat astride what seemed a large urn with oriental designs covering it. She had had to lift her gown off in order to use this urn, and her underthings, which were copious, were pulled down and in disarray all around her. Her breasts were held in by a white bodice, laced tight but with the top few stays undone. Her breasts were larger than they'd seemed at the table, and milky white. Her face betrayed no intelligence of my standing near, so I assumed I was safely invisible behind the door. I was both repulsed and attracted as I stood there. I felt arousal, and in the privacy of that moment, was not too disgusted with myself for feeling it.

I imagined opening the door so she could see me—watching her.

It was monstrosity within me, this fantasy I had. It was cruel and ruthless and yet provided me with a sense of power and pleasure.

I imagined tearing the bodice from her, ripping out the stays, grinding my face into those virginal breasts while I took her breath away with my thrusts.

And then as I imagined all this, I drew a quick breath.

Sitting on the urn, she seemed to glance up at me for a moment.

Had she seen me?

I drew back quickly.

I quietly walked back through the bath area, and nearly bounded down the stairs. I decided to use the privy outside, after all. My heart beat rapidly. Had she seen me watch her? If so, what had she felt? Had she felt terror? Had she been intrigued? Why had I turned to this perversion, this fantasy, while a fine young lady had relieved herself? What disgusting nature had I plumbed within my own flesh?

But when I returned to the table, just in time for the dessert course, she sat there and engaged me in conversation as if she had not seen or heard a thing. Was this social hypocrisy? Or had she truly not known that a man stood staring at her in her most private of moments, a man who imagined ruining her for the future respectable marriage that her life required? Had she known that someone with the heart of a monster lurked nearby?

4

Finally, the awful dinner was over. The men retired to the library for cigars and brandy. I was just sober enough to request tea instead. I sat through the long, endless jokes meant to be considered off-color, but which seemed tame and pointless to me. The men spoke of business dealings, but not directly to me, as I was not then, nor would I ever, be part of their world.

James winked at me, at nearly eleven o'clock, and Wendy tapped his feet impatiently. "We've got a soiree to go to," James whispered to me, glancing at the other men.

"Where are you young gallants off to?" the old admiral asked, cigar smoldering, a slight red line of Madeira on his white mustache.

Wendy quickly said, "The Alfred, I think."

"Or Boodle's," James added, mentioning one of the more famous and distinguished gentleman's clubs.

"Boodle's? It's popular as ever? I went there as a young man, as well," the old man said.

But when we were out the door, I asked James if this Boodle's or the Alfred were our destinations.

"Those are for the elderly," James said, clapping a hand over my shoulder once we were safely outside, away from the chatter of the social gathering. "We're going to a dangerous place called the Pandemonium. There are some delicious whores I want you to meet."

5

Off in a rush, fresh air and rain greeted us, as the hired cab trotted us down to the third ring of hell, the despicable, smelly end of the city, through alleys and byways unknown to me. When I looked out into the night as the cab slowed, I felt foreboding in this area. The streets were crowded with slatterns and urchins, like insects crawling along a feeble light in the darkness. Yet despite the stink and the crush of humanity, I preferred this—the thing itself, life, the underbelly, and the mud beneath the rock—to the soft eiderdown pillow of the rich, smothering me in my sleep.

We were all drunk, and I felt apprehensive about following my fellows in through the narrow alleyway, down the cobblestones, heaps of dung just off the main path, to a door that was little more than splintered wood.

"Here you go, Just," Wendy said, stuffing pound notes into my hand. "You'll need this. Do not give me a look about it, take it, it is mine to give and yours to have."

"Dear God," James said, with a sour grimace, "it smells like spume in here. The humanity of it all is stifling."

"And yet," Wendy added, his arm over my

261

shoulder, a bottle of port in his hand. "It is strangely enticing."

"Welcome to the sewer of flesh," James said to me, and pulled me inside the nasty place.

PART TWO

DEBAUCHERY

These metaphysics of magicians,
And necromantic books are heavenly!
—Christopher Marlowe, Dr. Faustus

Source of all life, Mother Death,
Plunder me.
Plunder my offering.
Tear the hole of my soul.
Cut me down as I stand in your presence.

—Justin Gravesend,
from the poem/prayer "Opening the Gate"

Chapter Seven

The Brothel

1

I entered what I thought was like the *cloxa maxima*, the name given to the Roman sewer system of ancient days, for the stench was great, and yet the allure was undeniable.

A large woman, laughing as if life were its own joke, greeted us just inside the door. A cigarillo tipped from the edge of her red lips, and she greeted us as the Mother of Harlots that she was, with her bounteous breasts bare and the stays of her corset open and free, only slightly cupping the monstrous tits, their nipples rouged, one with a small garnet-stone pierced in the aureole. She welcomed my friends and reached over to hug me, smothering me with mounds of bosom, which smelled of ginger and sweat. "You're cold, m'dear, but we'll warm you up soon enough."

James and Wendy were laughing riotously as

they saw me turn blue from lack of breath. "Meet Lady Caroline, Justy," James chortled. "Lady Caroline, you mustn't smother the gentleman!"

When she drew back, she introduced us to the boy-servant she called her helper. "This is Rabbit. Rabbit, I want you to take our guests back into the salon. These are gentlemen, and I expect you should watch how they behave if you wish to move up in this world."

Rabbit, the small young man, could not have been more than eighteen, but he looked as if he had aged to sixty. I had heard in my biology studies that there was a rare disease that could do this. I assumed that keeping the company this unfortunate must needs keep for his work, he might be one of the many bastards born of whores in the city, and the curse of his mother had descended to him, leaving him a child who would die before he was a man. His skin was wrinkled, and his eyes sunken, as if he had never been truly young in all his life.

I soon learned the reason for his nickname, for he hopped about as he went, and I began to see him less as an unfortunate, and more as someone who had found the world in which he might thrive, despite the vagaries of an indifferent deity.

2

We followed hopping Rabbit through this house of ill repute, its maze-like rooms decorated with imitation frescos of satyrs with enormous penises jabbing helpless nymphs and dryads, as well as wall murals that seemed from India, of turbaned and silk-clothed rajahs with engorged members tipped like red arrows pressing into the yielding caverns of veiled women who kissed and pinched each others' breasts. The colors, in the flickering wall lamps, were muted browns and yellows and reds. In the wide rooms off the hall, gentlemen with their trousers unbuttoned and their blousy shirts thrown open, their collars hanging at their shoulders, grasped the available female flesh— the wenches and unfortunates whose chief talent involved their tongues and their hips, and it struck me, as it had before, how pleasure for one was rarely pleasure for another. Surely these slatterns and strumpets could not enjoy this work, this labor, any more than I enjoyed my early work in the colliery, among the spoil heaps and caverns. But the gentlemen did not mind, for they were lost in their own ecstasies, as they squeezed and rammed and tasted. Even walking down the hallway, poorly lit by mutton-candle sconces, I heard the moans and cries of human lust. In the flickering candlelight, I saw the forms against the wall, men pressed against women, men against men, but all in shadow, all not quite seen, and a strange slowness to their movements as if they were snake charmers, careful not to make a wrong move for fear of getting bitten. Because of the brandy I'd consumed that night, I couldn't quite focus on these actors of the libido. We pushed past them to another doorway, and through this door, we came to a large room—a salon, filled with overstuffed lounges and a bar at one end. Here it was a bit more dignified, although the décor and the mode of dress left no question about what the business of the house might be. The walls had paintings of naked women, their legs lazily spread, or classical themes of Bacchus chasing a wood nymph, and a few of Leda and the Swan by various artists of lessening talents.

"Sir," Rabbit said, cupping his small hands together.

James whispered in my ear, "Generosity to the poor, mate."

I reached into my pocket and withdrew four pence.

Rabbit's eyes lit up when he saw what landed in his hands.

"I say," Wendy said. "Don't give too much. You'll ruin these people. The whores are no more than three quid, if that."

"Two for five," James added, gleefully.

In the salon, the women were bare-breasted like the proprietress, and walked around, amazons on the hunt, carrying pints and pitchers of bitter and ale. The men sat, talking with each other, laughing at jokes, or playing cards at one of several low tables. In some respects, it was a more democratic society than the dinner party I'd just left, for women smoked and dealt cards, and I overheard one conversation where one of the whores spoke about news of the famine in Ireland. The men were of the upper classes, all, dressed as if for a fancy ball, and looking as wealthy rakes might when relaxed: as if the need for relief and release was tantamount to reaching heaven itself.

Rabbit hopped off to get me a beer, but I had one from a mustachioed whore faster than he could retrieve a drink. When he returned, I took the pint from him, and set it down. "Here," I said, offering another tuppence. "For your trouble."

"Thankee, sir."

"Rabbit, can you tell me something?"

"Sir?"

"Why is this place called the Pandemonium?"

"It is because it is, sir."

"Pandemonium is a peculiar name," I said. "It implies the devil."

"The master," he said, an impish look to his aged face.

"The master?"

"The one what owns it." Then, in a broken Cockney, Rabbit told me of the man who, sitting in a corner of the salon, was the richest man in all the world, richer than the queen. He had his wealth because he sold his soul to the devil. "We all knows it," Rabbit said. "But we likes bein' 'ere, and we don't mind the devil so long's the marks come in reg'lar."

I paid Rabbit a one-pound note, and he nearly kissed my hand over it. He went hopping off, happy that he'd earned in a moment more than he probably had in the past month or more.

Then I turned back to watch this so-called "master."

3

He was not like the others. Yes, he had an air of the aristocrat about him. He held his cane and gloves just so, and his hair was cut in the current fashion, and he had the long unremarkable face of the city gentleman.

But he was more alive in his eyes than everyone else sitting in that salon.

He wasn't there for a girl.

He was there for all of it. A whoremaster? Hardly. This man looked as if he could indeed sell his soul to the devil.

And the devil would want it.

I immediately wanted to meet him. James was stunned that I was not ready to grab a wench and take off for one of the private rooms upstairs. "Take two or three," he said as he pressed coins into my hand. "These girls will let you do anything you like." Then he said something that only struck me as odd later, as the night wore on. He winked and said, "All right then, mate, you shall find us when you need us. But you must try the whores here. They're fabulous creatures."

But I had no interest. If I wanted sex, I had my life for it. I wanted to meet the man whose dark eyes seemed to know something more about the world than I could learn on my own.

4

I have learned since that his ability had to do with what is called "the glamour," and that is a level of connectedness to the world that one only gets when under the influence of a particular narcotic, Lotos (not "Lotus," but certainly meant in the same spirit as the classical lotus of Homer's poem), in the parlance of the sect that harvests its nectar and administers it to those willing to risk using it, in small doses. But then I just knew that he was magnetic, and I wanted to know something of what he knew.

Without even being sure how I moved so swiftly to him, I stood before him, offering my hand. "Sir." I bowed slightly, feeling as if he were some prince of the realm.

He waved me off, a dismissive gesture with his hands. "I'm busy," he said.

"May I . . . may I sit here?" I indicated the seat beside him.

"If you wish," he said.

"I am Justin."

He nodded but said nothing. He kept staring at the others. I looked among them, and saw my friend Wendy grab a girl's breast, stroking it lightly. Then they went off through a second door, presumably to the upstairs rooms.

"All of them," the man said, "animals." I would like to say that this distinguished-looking gentleman had an equally distinguished voice, but in fact, he had a slight Cockney accent, but with an upper-crust twist. "Look at them. Feeding on each other. Bloodsuckers. Wasting their energies."

"You own this establishment?"

"You're from the country."

"Yes, sir," I said. "Manchester."

"No, I mean the country. Wales?"

I nodded. "The Northeast part."

"A collier."

"I was, sir."

"Are you the one I was brought here to meet?"

"Sir?"

"I was brought here tonight to meet someone," he said. "I was called."

"Sir, it was not I. I only arrived in London today, and am staying with friends."

"Ah," he said. "Your friends are here. They bring you to London to see this. The carnival. The flesh pit."

"No, sir. They brought me here to enjoy a few days respite from studies."

"A student? I should've guessed. You are a poor boy who has clawed his way, using his talents, using whatever is at his disposal, to rise in the world. But this world, this world you see, has no interest in your concerns. Tell me, boy, why aren't you coupling with one of these ladies? Why aren't you in the hall, or upstairs on a sodden mattress, your cannon roaring? Isn't this the sport you students enjoy so much?"

"I don't find this interesting," I said. "And I'm not a boy."

"Of course you're not, not like our little friend Rabbit," he said. He reached over, and pressed his finger just under my chin. He felt my pulse. I could feel my heart beat beneath his cold finger. I felt wicked for thinking it, but when he touched me, I experienced a strange and lewd excitement, as if he were forcing some intimacy upon me that both felt good but also felt wrong. As he leaned into the lamplight, I gasped. His face was a smooth alabaster—like a statue, white and cold, and yet handsome in a smooth, unnerving way. His lips seemed to have the pinkness of youth, and his nose, aquiline and noble. Only his eyes, in the flickering light, put fear into me, for the pupils were dilated, engorged and blackened. I will admit that I had only seen this on one human being before:

A corpse.

In my brief study of medicine, I had gotten close to a corpse after examination, and its open eyes were like this. When I asked why, the surgeon told me that it had to do with the trauma that had caused the man's death as well as some unusual chemical poured into the eye after death. It made the eye look as if it were a large shiny black marble.

"You are twenty. Your name is Justin. Justin Grave. Graverson." Then he let go. He smiled, slightly. "You are him who I was meant to meet here. You are my reason for haunting this place. Shall I tell you something about yourself, Justin? Shall I? Shall I tell you that I know your soul, and that you have given yourself to pleasures and to death, and you long for something that cannot be held in our world, but only in the next?"

I listened to him with a sense of dislocation. He seemed familiar to me now, as if he were my father, but the kind father I had not yet met. He seemed someone to whom I wanted to be near, to touch in some way. My arousal for the whores (for it would be ridiculous for me to here deny that the sight of the nearly naked women, their bosoms rising and falling as they laughed in the arms of men who stroked them, would not bring me to full goat-hood—my phallus straining against my trousers—as the whole world now seemed as a flesh carnival made only for my enjoyment) had heated my skin and flooded my mind with visions and a long-forgotten taste of a woman's Venus delta.

And the man who sat with me now, speaking in sonorous tones, with the eerily pale skin and eyes like stone, seemed part of the arousal itself.

"You were born to what you are about to receive, my boy. You were meant for this, for my world, for the future."

I sighed when he spoke, no doubt like a girl in love, because all my life I had wanted to be destined for something greater than where I had been born. All my life, I had felt that missing thing, that half of me, my twin, my other, the one who knew of me and yet had not reached me.

This man, much older than myself, and yet still young and virile and masterful, might be that one. I do not write here of a sexual nature, but of a compelling magnetism that I could not resist, nor would I, even if given the choice.

"I am your Master," he said. "I am he who is meant to initiate you into the truth of who you are."

In that moment, I believed him, and accepted the adventure he offered.

Then he took his gloves up, and rose. "Come with me, Justin. I want to show you something. Something extraordinary."

Chapter Eight

The Three Rooms

1

The smells of the rooms were intensely conflicted: perfumes the likes of which had not scented harems outside of Araby, mingled with the stench of human sweat and sexual congress. If one believes that fornication is pleasure, one only need dispute this when smelling its effects with many fornicators doing what they love the most. It is the human body at its most pained. And yet its most pleasured. We watch the act of fertility with disdain. It brings us to the level of dogs. And yet within each act, if we are the participants, the excitement and feelings make us believe we are entering the pure realm of godhood. So the participants in these rooms, and in the recesses of the corridors, must have felt their urgent mission of lust to be uplifting, afterward looking at their compatriots, they surely must've been struck by the futility and the filth of life itself, and the source of life, the act of the phallus invading the opening of another, which then engulfed and devoured the manhood. And this is what I observed with my guide pointing out the more lewd and twisted body formations around us.

I followed him like a puppy in need of a master, through several rooms, passing by mattresses and writhing bodies. "There are three rooms I want you to see tonight. You will observe those things that you may find most repulsive, perhaps," he said. "Does that frighten you?"

"No," I said, and meant it, for I had developed a keen curiosity about him and this place. Truth be told, I had dreams that were much more lurid than even the heaving bodies that slammed and pressed each other in the dank corners of this brothel. Nor, I admit, was I a stranger to the whore, for in Manchester, with friends, I had visited them once or twice, although in circumstances much less elaborate than the Pandemonium.

He led me first into one large room, upon which was a sumptuous bed. The room was well-lighted, and in one corner an African serving girl, coifed in the older style of powdered wig and a lady's riding suit, played the clavier near the entrance, a lively tune with an unusual rhythm. When I entered the room, she alone turned to look at me, and I discovered that it was not a girl at all, but a young man dressed as a girl.

2

I passed this musician and stepped in farther, for it seemed there was a small crowd therein. Over the bed, a great mirror. Beside the bed, two manservants, wearing only trousers, sat holding long, intricately carved pipes that released a thin, lazily swirling smoke. These were opium pipes. Around the bed sat several well-dressed young ladies and older men, stout and puffy of face. A peculiar sweet smell was in the air, mixed with something like wormwood. The audience looked as if they were meant to be at the opera. Instead, they watched the spectacle on the bed.

The servants' masters were in the bed, pleasuring a wench sandwiched between them, their shirts only half torn from their bodies. Buttocks thrust into her from before and behind. I was repulsed by this public display more than the activities seen in the other rooms. There was a strange and disturbing refinement to it. These acts seemed less about the pleasure and more about the spectacle. And yet I, like the other spectators, wanted to watch. The moans of lust became loud, and seemed like chants to me, and then in the mirror above, I saw the faces of the participants and recoiled.

My school chums, James and Wendy, pressed

into the whore, their hair flying, their eyes rolled up so much into their sockets that all I saw was whiteness. Worse than my friends taking their carnal pleasures, the woman in between them was none other than the angel of purity I had seen at the dinner party:

Anya, the one whom James intended to marry.

The lady I had spied upon in her private moments.

It looked—if this scene were to be believed—as if my friends were taking their liberties with her just as I had dreamed of doing.

Surely, I thought, this was a charade for my benefit; this was a whore who had been made up to look like that most chaste young maiden. Surely this could not be the virgin who at the dinner table was fascinating with art and politics and seemed so much finer than her dinner companions, whose milk-white breasts had invitingly been displayed for me, briefly, without her knowledge.

Behind me, I heard my guide's voice, "Do you see the beauty of it? And do you see the monstrosity?"

I nodded. With much sadness, I said, "Is this the extraordinary thing you wanted me to witness? The debauchery of an innocent at the hands of two libertines?"

"No, my friend. The extraordinary is yet to come. This is the world, and it is no better than this bedroom," he said. "Most human beings watch those with power take their pleasures from the innocent and unknowing. She is drugged, you see. She is innocence. They are all guilty, not just the two men, but those who watch and smile. The world is full of spectators, watching the debauchery of others. Watching and applauding its corruption. Look at them, with their fascination at seeing this event. Who in the world is not like this, willing to sit in judgment in the bedroom of others, to clap and hoot and live only through the eyes and not through the soul, and enjoy the humiliation of innocence? The lady in question does not even know she is here. She is dreaming, perhaps. She is not aware of her surroundings. Tomorrow, she shall awaken in her bed, knowing what has happened, seeing these same men and women in her daily life, not being certain if she experienced a nightmare or if, in fact, she has merely been a puppet in their despicable fantasy." Then, he touched my shoulder. "But come, Justin. There is more to see here."

I went with him, drunk, not understanding, not knowing if this were all a lie, a show, if Anya hadn't been at the dinner that night, a whore dressed up as a lady, or if she were a lady, drugged, kidnapped and brought into this den of depravity by my two rakish chums who, in my mind, seemed common criminals for this terrible show. Confusion took over my mind, and I could not believe that James and Wendy were the sorts to do this to a young lady, nor would I believe

that Anya was a whore who pretended to society.
I began to wonder if something of the poppy had
not been slipped into my own drinks that night.

And yet I went with the owner of the Pandemonium, out into the corridor, and down a dimly lit
hallway.

3

Into the next room we went, and this one was
much smaller than the one previous. Here, there
was nothing, nor was there anyone but a small
figure, cloaked in some sort of black cape, bent
down in the far corner of the room.

"Go to," he said.

I went over to the figure, and saw that it was
not a person at all, but a carved stone statue of a
saint in an aspect of prayer.

I turned to my guide, wondering.

"This is God," he said.

"This is not God."

"He is in this room, and this is His miracle. A
stone image of His work. The image of man. In
the image of God. Do you feel Him? Smell Him?
Can He be in this room in a house among whores
and thieves and drunkards?"

"They say that He can be anywhere."

"Then He is here. This is His room. But where
are his worshippers? They are elsewhere, they
surround him in other rooms, obeying the laws of
the flesh rather than His laws."

"Why do you show me this?"

"It is to show you that even in the midst of the worst of humanity," the gentleman said, "God does nothing. God cares little. Only this statue sits, bent at prayer, hoping to become something other than stone."

I laughed, enjoying the joke, feeling somehow less disturbed. So this was a carnival, a play, a show for me to enjoy. I wondered if all new visitors to the Pandemonium were treated to this grand tour. I thought of my father, and how he would've cried out to heaven to save himself from such heathen and godless behavior, and it made me warm to think that I had ended up at the same place he would've considered a vision of hell.

I left the strange little room and its odd statue, and followed him down the last several feet of the corridor.

4

The hall ended abruptly.

"What of the last room? The third?" I asked.

The gentleman then produced a key from his waistcoat, and proceeded to open a door that I would not have noticed had he not known where to turn the key. The door, smaller than most, opened on a long staircase downward. I had to crouch down to fit through the door, as did he. There were lamps lit along the wooden stairs, and again, I followed him, this time into the bowels of the building.

When we reached the bottom step, it seemed darker there, and I hesitated before taking another step forward.

Gently, he took my hand. In the shadows, I could barely see his face. "You must come, Justin. This is why we had to meet. This is what drew me here tonight, and you."

He led me through the shadow of this underground lair, and soon enough we came to another door, behind which were voices.

"Where are we going?" I asked.

"To speak with the Dead," he said.

Visionary 3

Now, I can see them better—there are four of them, coming from the burning forest, loping toward me with their teeth showing yellow and sharp, and the puffed skin around their eyes, their many eyes, red and wounded, and I continue to batter at the door to keep it open, to keep the portal wide. I hear the moans of my chosen one, but I continue to tear at him, to scrape my fingers across his flesh, as the creatures—the gods—come to me, their arms raised in joy and hunger, their nether mouths opening, revealing shiny black teeth beneath the folds of their bellies.

Tentacles of pleasure shoot from me, like light from pinholes in a shadowbox, I AM BECOMING! I AM TRANSFORMING FROM MY FLESH OUTWARD! My subject, beneath me, held and clawed by me, feels the tendrils of my energy pressing along his flesh, into the soft lubricity of his skin, which is shimmering like a lake, and rippling as if hundreds of pebbles are being thrown into it, but not pebbles, my tentacles, my slim quivers, my quills, thrust into his back and thighs, along his shoulders, into his neck, curving around to enter the holes of his ears, and, like a starfish opening a clam, they reach around to his mouth, to his clenched teeth, and pry him open there, to enter him, to take the sacrifice offered, to possess him completely.

The burning within the pathways of my body is heaven itself, is a feeling of well-being and weightlessness, and I as I begin to possess him, to tear him, to gnaw at him, and the gods approach, and reach for his eyes.

Chapter Nine

The Room of Sighs

1

I laughed when we entered the large, well-appointed room. I knew now I must have been drugged in my cups, for I felt wonderful and light, and resisted nothing.

Like the upstairs rooms, it was lit with cheap candles secured onto the walls, and a mural of debauchery encircled all within the room. But these debaucheries seemed less innocent than those in the front hallways of the Pandemonium. The paintings were of knights, in full black armor, their codpieces arched and made to look very much like their lances, their gauntlet-covered hands pressing deep into the openings of a young lass, one at her mouth, one at each ear, and the greatest knight of all, his hand over her maidenhead. There was nothing pleasurable about the image, nor did it incite my imagination, for there was something wholly disgusting about the knights and their defenseless victim, whose naked body was painted with symbols of an occult nature. In another part of the mural, a man was tied to a cross that was shaped like an X, and two women stood near him with small knives, having just made incisions along his spinal column. They were flaying him alive, and the look on the young man's face was one of a martyred saint experiencing ecstasy, while his torturers wore expressions of beatific grace. Along another wall, men copulated with fantastic beasts, including gorgons and harpies and unicorns and gryphons. In one panel, a gryphon held a man down with its talons and took him from behind, an enormous and scaled phallus pressed into the curves of the man's buttocks; in another, a unicorn's horn pressed into the folds of a woman's innards while a man, standing over her, pressed a small dagger into his own belly, a full erection beneath this. Other creatures populated the mural, including beautiful women whose faces had been obliterated into whiteness, whose nipples had become open mouths with rows upon rows of teeth, and whose nether parts were as those of baboons, the female organ large and red and engorged, or men with the heads of fish, five arms, all clutching some otherworldly vine from which grew a small blue flower, their arms ending in tentacles and small whips of hair. It was wondrous and terrible. The images were nightmarish, and yet strangely beautiful, but did not match the spectacle within the room itself.

2

Writhing on the floor, an orgy of flesh.

It was not the Dead who were there, but several young men and women, all quite beautiful and well-groomed. They fondled each other on several mattresses. On straw mats in a corner, men lay down on pillows while young women offered them the opium pipe. Some seemed to have an aristocratic bearing, the shiny hair of the rich, the clean, well-oiled skin, the slender, the athletic. Others less so, darker, with a Celtic look to them, smaller, and yet no less appetizing to consider as they rutted and rolled. It was yet another level of the brothel, and I was a little relieved when I realized that this was yet another metaphorical hell, as the first two rooms he had shown me had been of Social Hypocrisy, I assumed, and then of the Silence of God. This must be The Sins of the Flesh, and it was a good deal merrier and more alluring than the other rooms.

"Do you like them?" my guide asked, pointing out two women frolicking on some pillows, tenderly kissing each other, and patting each other's buttocks. Isolated from the outside world like this, truly, I felt my animal nature take over, and that growling beast came out.

"Yes," I replied, or perhaps only thought I

replied. My breathing slowed as if the very air I needed were being denied me. I felt my body more than my mind.

"Go on," he said. "They're yours. Go to them."

In other circumstances, I might've run from that room, but I was still a young man, and my libido had been aroused by the entire venture into this playground of the devil. Furthermore, there was something of the somnambulist about this man. I felt as if I were in his power, or else I had given my will over to him for this adventure. I imagined this was the feeling of Adam, taking the apple to his lips, knowing that it was forbidden and terrible, understanding that there would be consequences and attacks of conscience on the morrow. But the allure and the opportunity. I had nothing drawing me back. No woman, no obligation, no sense that this would even be known outside this room.

My member was hard and whatever power Nature has over any one of us, She had over me at that moment more powerfully than I had ever before felt it. I felt that I would die right then if I didn't find a warm harbor in the hips of those women, that I needed the acceptance of the naked human flesh, the sea of rapture awaited.

3

I waded through the writhing bodies—the two men who caressed a woman who arched her back and pressed both sides of herself into their lower regions. On a mattress, a young man with a long member thrust himself quickly and with accompanying groans, into a woman with wide, inviting hips. Two men lay together, stroking each other, while a woman kissed each of them passionately on the lips. I felt a strange, compelling want, a hunger, to let go of any restraint within my mind. I was in London, and moreover, I was in an underground chamber of sin, lust, and pleasure. Further, I was somehow within the grasp of my puppeteer-host, and felt as if I were meant to perform in this play before him.

My mind seemed to turn off to some degree, for this kind of sexual play appealed to the libido and not the conscious mind. It all seemed as if it were permissive, allowed, and I went to the two soft women, and pressed myself against them, between them. My fine clothes peeled away, layer by layer, my neck held and rubbed and kissed. They licked me and caressed me, both of their mouths going to my privates, their bodies turned around, and I tasted them and smelled their essence, and it was as if I had smoked the opium myself, for I felt my mind somehow dissolve, like the rain outside. My mind was no longer located beneath my scalp, but was in my pores, in my fingers, along my thighs, in my toes—as if every part of my being were thinking by way of touching.

Others joined us. I felt foggy and distant, although the impulses in my skin seemed to grow. Every touch was an awakening to something new. I felt the rough touch of a young man my own age as he grasped me around the waist. I did not register revulsion, nor did I wish him not to hold me thus. And the women, my hands between their thighs, a whisper of obscenity in my ear, someone taking each of my toes in her mouth and holding it as if it were a rare dessert. I have never felt such delight in perversion as I did then, and if part of me felt this were wrong; if my religious upbringing had any warning bell going off, I somehow let it ring without responding to it. The pleasure, again. The pleasures of carnality were upon me, and I was a reveler. I rolled in this garden of ecstasy, feeling caresses and thrusts and mouths and warmth and wetness, all the while my mind seemed to turn as black as the skies over my home village, a seeping darkness that betokened nothing, while my sensory organs flickered and sputtered with a sense of being extinguished and awakened, over and over again.

I forgot my guide, my host, the mysterious gentleman, until the banquet of sensual delights was devoured.

Then, awakening from the slow withdrawal from pleasure and flesh, that terrible cracked feeling as if one is broken and now needs mending, I saw him standing over me. He had been watching.

I felt naked and ashamed, and reached for my shirt. I became aware of the filthiness of the act, of the uncouth nature of my own body and its compulsions. As I wrapped my shirt about my shoulders, I noticed the others.

I tell you, I saw the most terrifying thing that could be seen at that moment.

Not the beautiful men and women of this paradisiacal brothel, this private room within the rooms.

But corpses.

I knew a corpse well enough from the laboratory, from the medical amphitheater in Manchester.

The skin, the signs of putrefaction, the slightly bloated nature, the eyes, the way the musculature had changed owing to the lack of that spark of life.

They lay around me, and I could identify each one. The buttocks of the beautiful man with the gentle lips. The twin, slightly lopsided breasts of the young lady with the curled hair, her ribbons falling around her Botticelli face and shoulders. The two dark-haired men pressed, still, so close to their lovely companion, her mouth still gaping in a parody of orgasmic joy. Or, perhaps, a scream.

Those I had only just left off embracing.

The women and the men, naked and beautiful, and so dead that their skin was of a bluish hue, and their eyes, staring at nothing, as if they'd only just come from the arms of Mother Death.

4

"Did you love them?" he asked.

I sat shivering, unsure of my surroundings, unsure if I had been drugged or somehow tricked and these were not lifeless beings but dolls, or actors playing tricks.

"The Dead can love," he continued. "They are here, all the time. They speak to us, but we do not hear them. And we can speak to them."

"Who are you?" I asked, feeling as if I had just crawled into a room in my mind that I might never open again. Trying to make sense of this night before insanity took hold, before the disease of what I had done grasped my heart.

"I am your Master," he said. "And was called by one who is Dead to find you."

Then he held something up before me. I did not recognize it at first.

"I raised him up and spoke to him, and he brought me the secrets of the other realm," he said. From his bundle, he produced the small skull, cleaned of grit and hair and filth. "He brought you and I together. You will wake tomorrow, this will be a dream, but if your soul finds no rest, you will find me again. You will find the one you have sought your whole life."

At the back of the skull, the part of it that had been smashed in by some small knife or other tool.

My brother's bones.

Chapter Ten

The Seeker

1

Then, the smell of pine and sweet treacle in my nose, a gaseous mixture of some sort, I blacked out.

2

I awoke to a strange rumbling, my head pounding. I had been drugged, I thought, and somehow my dream of orgy and its stygian aftermath was simply induced by opium, or perhaps the brandy mixed with some foreign liqueur. Brothels were notorious for this kind of thing, and I could not have expected anything less from a house of ill repute called the Pandemonium.

When I opened my eyes, the sunlight itself seemed like hammers pounding at me. I lay in the bed to which I must have been ushered earlier in the day while passed out—at the house at Regent's Park owned by my chum James. I tried to retrace my last memories of the night. All I could recall was the terrible scene of horror, surrounded by the beautiful bodies of the dead, and the feeling that I had been fondling, holding, licking, and even physically entering them. I knew of stories of necrophiliacs, those who enjoyed copulation with corpses, and I shuddered to think of what I might have done. Or dreamed. I felt waves of revulsion go through me. I lay a long time, clutching my pillow and bedclothes, looking up at the ceiling of my room, trying to understand how I could've had such a dream, or such a strong feeling that it had not been a dream at all.

Yet surely, I argued within myself, you've had nights of drunken wanderings in which you imagined things done that may not have been done. Or done things without knowing you had done them, later. Surely, this had been such a night. How many brandies had been drunk before dinner? How much wine with dinner? And the port afterward? And the Madeira? The pint of ale at the brothel, surely I had at least one while there? How could I possibly have experienced the feeling of those women touching me, urging me into their bodies, and how could I have allowed a man to grasp me about the waist without fighting him? Surely this was a dream that meant I should not drink so much in one night!

After several minutes of convincing myself of the impossibility of the previous night's revel, I rose, trembling from the effects of too much alcohol, and stumbled and fumbled my way to the chamber pot in the well-appointed bath down the hall.

3

The day was a normal one. James and Wendy, too, were suffering the effects of the previous night. When we sat in a parlor, speaking of school and sports, I could not get the images of them out of my head, of their ecstasy and grimace, their groans of animal conquest as they plundered the angel of virtue, fair Anya. Yet I had the distinct impression that they were none the worse, whether it had happened or not. And to be sure, I became convinced by the minute that it could not have happened, for they certainly would be mentioning it now, or alluding to it in some way. To provoke this, I brought up Anya's name, mentioning her beauty, and James laughed and told me that she was not nearly as beautiful as the whores had been the previous night.

"Do you remember whom you bedded?" I asked.

"The sordid details, mate?" James laughed, heartily, and then groaned because even his laugh caused him distress, he was suffering so from the effects of drink. "I took two for my fun, and they were lovely girls, but this is not a subject for discussion." Here, his voice quieted, because of the nearby servants. "Suffice it to say, it was sweet and over too fast."

"And you?" I asked my other friend.

"I don't talk of this stuff," Wendy said. "Say, shall we go to the opera tonight?"

"Opera bores me," James said. "What about the Blackfriars?"

"Wonderful," Wendy said. He turned to me, "The Blackfriars Club is a sporting place. You will love it, Justin."

They continued their conversation, turning toward horses and their plans for the next few days, but my mind was elsewhere. The three rooms, the orgy, all of it had seemed so real, but it was as if it were a truth of night, whereas daylight brought a different truth.

I had the unsettling feeling as the day wore on that there was truth to my memory, or at least a beveled truth, bending the last of my memory round the curved edges of my sense of reality.

I began to remember further details of the night, and took leave of my companions and set off for a walk through the gardens of the park, just off the square. It was a gorgeous late spring afternoon, and the park was empty save for ladies walking in groups or nursemaids with their charges at the benches, feeding ducks or buying sugar candy from the vendors. As I watched them, I began to feel what I can only describe as deviant urges. I observed the young ladies, and wished to, in that perfect day, grab them and tear their fineries from them, exposing their white flesh to the burning sun, and taking them right there, in front of the matrons and the nursemaids. Taking them, like some human monster, and enjoying their cries and whimpers. It was a terrible self-loathing that then came over me, that I could watch these decent ladies and imagine pummeling them from mouth to fundament, and savoring their degradation. It was disgusting, and I set off from the park, profoundly disturbed by my dream from the previous night, and from my monstrous thoughts along the garden path.

I knew I was not a monster, and yet I found myself uncomfortable in my own skin.

4

A man may walk many miles in a few hours if he feels the devil at his heels.

I wandered the city, thinking I might need a church, although I tended to avoid them. Yet my upbringing, between my puritanical father and devoutly Catholic mother, could not be denied. I felt better in church, and felt I needed to go there to somehow purge myself of these unnatural feelings. I found a church on Gower Street and entered straightaway. It was empty and cold, but the large crucifix at the front, by the altar, and the windows that depicted the saints and martyrs, brought me some comfort. I went and sat down, and prayed a bit, or tried. But my mind kept returning to sexual force and power, and a feeling of wanting to go into the streets and grab the first man or woman there, and to lick a human ear while tearing at the fabric of trousers, or ripping the bodice from an unsuspecting and chaste maiden. I sat, aroused in God's house, and when I looked at the stained glass of the windows, I didn't see St. Francis praying with animals, but saw him, his monk's robes up around his waist, his enormous phallus rammed into the haunches of a donkey . . . or St. George, his lance going into not a dragon, but a crouching woman.

When I looked up at the cross, it was not Jesus I saw there, but my own father, and beneath him, my older sister Bathsheba, pleasuring him with her tongue. I am cursed! I railed within myself. Blasphemy comes out of my mind! Malicious pictures plague my thoughts!

What drug had been given me the previous night? I wondered. What madness and degeneracy had befallen me that I should see these visions? I covered my eyes, and then bit down hard on my lower lip, drawing blood, just to feel something, to know that I was real, and these mad thoughts and dreams were merely the result of poisoning of some sort.

When I opened my eyes, the church and its figures and windows had returned to their former sacred states.

I felt a sense of panic, as if God watched me now, in His house, watched and judged me, and worse, there was no forgiveness in this sense. I felt the thudding of my own heart in my chest, and wondered if this were what one felt just before death. I went out into the streets, which seemed desolate and unwelcoming. I ran down side streets as one afraid that the devil himself might be chasing me, were I to look back. Any stranger I saw seemed threatening, and I dared not look at women or men, for fear that I would inflict some diabolical act upon them.

I arrived at a public house and went in, thirsty and feverish. I bought several pints, and managed to drown some of my fear. The palpitations in my breast lessened.

I was surrounded by men very much like those from my home village—workmen from Scotland and Wales and the boroughs surrounding the city, tarred nearly black with pitch or coal dust, or covered with the white powder of plastering and bricklaying work. I felt a sense of calm.

After an hour or so, I went out into the now-twilight street, the first of the gas lamps being lit. The street narrowed, and I had a choice of going right onto a wide avenue, or to the left, into a side street with a shambles of lower-class apartments above steamy laundries and other vice houses. Although my conscious mind bid me go to the open boulevard, my body yearned for something in that darkening street, and as I walked, and walked some more, I realized that I had come, at last, to the alley in which stood the place called the Pandemonium.

I knew I had to enter it again.

5

When I crossed its threshold, I was taken aback.

It was empty.

Not empty as if it would later fill, as the midnight hour approached.

But empty as if it had never been full at all.

There were no signs in the corridor of the perverted couplings of men and women, nor of the carnival shouts of the fat, boisterous madam and her small assistant, Rabbit, who hopped along after her. It looked as if it had been abandoned for several days. I went room to room, remembering the shadow figures of heat and flesh, as Rabbit hopped ahead of me, taking me down the hall to the main salon. The murals remained on the walls, with their lewd figures and exotic positions. But it looked as if the place had not been occupied for months.

The door to the salon was missing, and as I stepped through the doorway, I saw that the place had been blackened by some kind of fire. The lamps were aglow, however, which meant that someone was there, someone still kept the lights going. I followed my memory trail into another hall, the way that the Master had taken me, but when I came to the place where the keyhole in the wall had been, there was nothing. Just wall. No door. No keyhole.

A dead end.

And then, someone grabbed me from behind, so swiftly that I got the wind knocked out of me. I held on to consciousness, and tried to fight my attacker with all I had.

Something soft—a kerchief?—went to my mouth. I smelled treacle and tar. It was that same sweet stink I'd detected the previous night. No matter how I fought, I felt myself grow weaker. It was not the smell of the sort of ether used in the medical laboratory, but it seemed to possess similar properties.

I awoke, possibly a few minutes later, in restraints, tied to a bed. I tugged at the strips of leather that held me at my wrists and ankles. A cloth had been wrapped tight over my mouth and jaw to keep me from speaking. I felt utterly powerless and vulnerable.

A voice in the shadowy darkness, the Master of the previous evening: "You have been the one sent to us, you have passed the first test of our Order, and now the most arduous of tests shall press you to the limit of your mind. Yes, against your will. For your will must be broken."

6

I cannot write here of the degradations that befell me in the dark pit of hell. I close my mind to its memory. To the prodding, and the pleasure that was terror, and what grasped me, and what gave itself to me, but it was all human, and all flesh, and of many types and aspects, a deviant, depraved sort of rape of my body and my will.

I fought against it, and yet, in my mind, my brother's bones were foremost.

How had this Master gotten them? What had they to do with me here?

I will say that at the end of the hours of pleasure and agony, I prayed for Death.

I prayed to join my brother.

Yet the worst came after.

A large, muscular man who looked as if he were a hired murderer came with two assistants whose faces had been painted egg-shell white, and began pressing needles into my flesh, slowly, methodically. I had no strength to fight, and I was afraid of their needles. They worked for many hours, tattooing images onto my back and buttocks and thighs, across my belly and chest, as well. When they were done, they drew out small tools—as if they were stone carvers. I tried to scream, but found that my throat was unable to emit more than a bleat. They had jewels and rings, and I felt the first pain in my left nipple as a long sharp needle went into it. Then a small ruby was attached, as a gypsy might wear a jewel in his ear. Other parts of my body were thus ringed and jeweled. The horrors of it were minor in the plan of all things. As I lay there, feeling the fire of needles and the cold touch of the rings as they pierced my body, I felt as if I would soon be killed. The pain was excruciating, and waves of unconsciousness befell me, although I awoke, blearily, through the worst of it, wanting to cry out in pain.

7

When it was over, I felt a warm hand untie me. Bare-breasted young women washed me with sponges, and anointed oils and perfumes on my skin and in my scalp. The tattoos were rubbed and gently dressed. Any wounds or cuts I had (for the small knives had sliced bits of my flesh beneath my arms, and near my thigh during a profoundly horrible hour) were taken care of, and a salve of some kind was rubbed into the reddened areas where my body had been pierced with jewels and small golden rings and round studs. My hair was trimmed, and my nails were buffed. I was clothed in a blouse that seemed to be made of gold, and in trousers that were thin and dark. Boots were brought, and slender maidens with veils over their faces pressed my feet into them. I was given water, which I drank greedily, and allowed a place to eliminate wastes; all the while my hands were not free, but held firmly. The degradations were continual, and yet there was a beauty to them. I felt like a child, just being born.

It was my rebirth.

Thus, dressed and cared for, I slept again until someone came and woke me.

8

When I awoke, I was in a very different place. It was a hall of sorts, not unlike the medical amphitheater in Manchester, where I watched corpses being dissected. I lay on a table, as would a corpse, my hands bound on my chest, my feet also bound, and these restraints connected by a leather strop between them to minimize my movements. Above me, in the tiered watchtowers of the theater, an audience. They wore great masks of birds and jackals and unicorns, and other fantastical or otherworldly sorts. Other than this, they were naked, and the men's phalluses were at erection, the women's legs were spread, their bodies reddened with face paint and rouge. As I noticed this fakery, I observed that the phallus of each man was not his own, but was also its own kind of mask—an exaggerated erection, designed by some perverse architect.

Standing before me, a man who wore a mask of a stag with great antlers, and his erection, too, was enormous, though I could see no outward sign that it was a counterfeit. His body was covered from chest to knees in an intricate mural of tattoos, images of creatures with mouths and tentacles, of orgies, and of faces too terrifying to describe here. It was an unspeakable canvas, and yet I could not help but look. As I watched the images, they seemed to move, and their lips opened, calling out, their arms wriggled along his skeletal muscularity. I noticed that his testicles and nipples, as well as navel, had the gemstones pressed into them, with a series of thin gold bands that hung from his member. It seemed both primitive, like islands found off the coast of a newly discovered world, with cannibals and headhunters, and yet, this was no doubt an Englishman, and when I heard his voice, I knew who it was.

It was the owner of the Pandemonium.

9

"You will die to the world," he said, his voice deep and calming. I felt at ease, despite my situation, as if something in his voice alone held power over me. "You will die as all men must die, but do not fear. You will this day find regeneration of body and soul, and you shall become one with us, the Golden Quivers of the Arrows of Apollo and of Baphomet and of Isis and of all who have been buried for thousands of years but who shall rise again through the chosen vessels."

Here, the others, watching me from above,

cried out some litany in a language that I had never before heard.

"You shall learn the secrets of Magick and the power of the Chimerical Realm, and gain dominion on this Earth, and speak with those who have spread themselves wide for the rape of Death," he said. Again, the litany rose from the crowd above us.

"You have been brought to us by a wandering spirit," he said. He held his hands out, and a woman who wore a swan mask approached, carrying a walnut box. She passed it to him, then receded into the shadows. He opened the box and held it aloft for the onlookers to see.

Then he drew a small skull out of it, setting the box down at the edge of the stone table on which I lay.

"The will of the gods is strong!" he shouted, and the onlookers cheered. "I spent three years seeking out the secrets of the dead, and happened by a cemetery, consecrated by the unholy. A woman of great wealth, her spirit trapped by the very secrets she wished to keep, lay in her grave, unable to find release. I unburdened her, sacrificing a young child I had met along the way, letting the child's blood run into the grave so as to raise the woman from the dead that she might whisper of her treasures. But instead, another came to me, one who died as a baby, came to me and told me of his brother, this man you see before you, this one who has been known as Justin Gravesend to the world, but shall, after his first death, be known by a new name to us, born within the Chymera." He brought the skull nearer my face. The stench was revolting; although perfumes had been applied to the skull, I could still scent disease and decay upon it. He pressed the skull to my lips, forcing me to kiss it, forcing the skull itself to kiss me, as well.

"Your brother told me of you. I knew that you were the one prophesied among the ancients and among our brethren, and the one of which many of the dead have spoken. Though you be a callow and pale youth who has ill-understood your role in the world, we have watched you, all of us!" He raised the small skull high, and the masked men and women cheered with renewed vigor. "You have been watched since that moment, followed, understood. We travel through the world, looking for such as you. We search for our messiahs who have been foretold from the lips of the gods themselves. And you shall be the very incarnation of Baphomet! You shall be the one to open the doorway to the Veil, and bring the Age of Gods upon us!"

Somewhere, a thin, reedy pipe began playing, and then a drum, its beat seeming ancient and strange. Not precisely musical or rhythmic, the watchers above us began a slow kind of dance that became a series of complicated, writhing embraces. This cult of orgiasts began their revels.

The Master of Ceremonies leaned over me, bringing the skull to my chest, and his lips to my ear. "Do not fear. Your brother had told me of the sign, and we have learned much of you. This has been ordained by the gods themselves."

He stood and set the skull in the wooden box.

A young woman came into view, through the incense mist, wearing a thin gossamer tunic, as if she were an actress in a Greek tragedy. She wore no mask, nor veil did she have, and I recognized her immediately.

With her own hands, she let slip her tunic and stood before the infernal congregation, naked.

It was Anya, the beautiful young lady from my recent dinner, and the same that I dreamed I had seen between my school friends in their whoring. The angel of purity who seemed to me now, a goddess from the netherworld itself. Her face was painted with occult symbols, and her breasts each sported the face of Baphomet. Her body scrawled across, in dark ink, words of another tongue. On her belly, above her delta, was the perfectly rendered drawing of the Master himself, who stood before her, his phallus erect and impossibly enormous, his teeth bared like a wolf's, his arms outstretched to clutch whomever pressed himself against this woman's body.

The Master of Ceremonies removed his mask, and as I knew, that alabaster face, and those beautiful gemstone eyes were behind it. He lifted Anya up and set her across my thighs. I struggled in my bonds, but found I had no movement. The more I struggled, the tighter my restraints became.

And there, on my body, the Master took her.

When he was done, he drew her up. He reached down to me to undo the restraints.

"This," he said, "is the first sacrifice that shall save you from the embrace of Death herself."

After my hands were free, and then my legs, he drew out that curious small blue flower and twirling vine from Anya's ringlets. He squeezed the petals into his hands. Then he pressed his moistened fingers, with the pollen smell of the flower, against my lips, my nostrils, my eyes. He rubbed the ointment—for that is what the crushed petals and vine became—across my body. Finally, with one thick droplet at the edge of his finger, he pressed this into my mouth, setting the warm burning bit of liquid on my tongue. It was sweet and bitter, reminding me of wormwood, and in consistency, viscous but smooth.

I felt its effects immediately, as if I had been hit, all at once, by a coach speeding by through a narrow alleyway. My body jerked as I felt the elixir's potency.

The shadows and the congregation faded, and a whiteness, as of paint coming from an invisible artist's brush across the air, swept along the edges of my vision. I experienced a clarity, as if my breathing had become deeper, more calming to me. The whiteness, at first in thick brush strokes, then in a kind of mist, enveloped us, and all I could see was Anya, and the Master of Ceremonies himself.

"Many die when they part the Veil," the Master said. "The Lotos is poison to all but the chosen. You must now make the six sacrifices if you wish to reach your heart's desire and your soul's longing."

As I was set free from all restraint, I felt something profound release from my mind, a great weight dropped, a mask being removed, like clouds moving out from a sun kept too long hidden from view.

As a dagger pressed into my hand, I had the first of my Visionaries, not merely visions, but a truly fundamental change in what I knew and experienced. I saw the woman before me, the woman I had known as Anya, the temple harlot, the unclean angel, the sacred whore, not as merely herself, but as the meat of the Gods.

I saw my flesh for what it was, the means of opening the sacrifice, of bringing the sacrifice into the realm of the divine.

The hole of flesh as a means of parting the Veil.

Surrounded by whiteness, I watched as small worms grew from my phallus, then from my arms, and from my mouth, a crawling mouth, a human mouth, a second set of teeth, yellowed and curved like the beak of a falcon, all snapping as the mouth emerged, lengthening. I was in communion with the gods. This was holy and not profane at all. These were the true commandments of the most holy: *that meat was the only food of the gods of power, and that I had truly been chosen, since the day of my birth, to perform this sacrifice of meat to the devourers that emerged from my own flesh.*

To rip open the hole.

To part the Veil.

To feed the gods.

Anya looked at me with her small *o* of mouth gasping like a fish that has been drawn by the fisherman from water. I went to encompass her, and I entered every part of her, my newborn tentacles finding the tiny pores of her skin and enlarging them as they burrowed beneath her flesh, my extended mouth ripping her lips, her gums, her tongue, her palate.

10

So the day and night passed, and I learned of the sacred texts. I read aloud from the Grimoire Chymera that had been passed from Hermes Trigestimus to the mortal Pandora to the Queen of Carthage, in whose library it was kept for centuries before the fires burned the magnificent Halls of Secrets of the Ancients. From there, it was taken into caves, into burial caverns, where from it, it is said the sacred Lotos grew, that flower of graveyards whose juice produces the poison Listanius, which kills a man on contact if he is not sanctified, or is the portal to the Veil for those who are chosen.

I spoke to the bones of my brother, and he told me of the secrets of Mother Death and the warmth of her bosom. The Master came to be known to me as the Necromancer, and he became more father to me than had my own father or my cherished uncle.

The Necromancer became my king.

But there was one knowledge I would only find, he told me, through my sacrifices. And so I procured my friends James and Wendy, and others of theirs, the old admiral, a young man I found on the streets, the proprietress of the Pandemonium, Lady Caroline. I opened each of them in turn and brought their meat to the gods.

11

And so, in my twenty-first year, I was reborn in the Chymera Magick. I had performed ritual murder and taken all manner of hallucinogenic drugs, including the Lotos that grew within the dankest of graves. I learned to raise the dead, and to speak with them, and learn of the treasures of the earth and of the air, and learned of their mysteries and their wisdoms. I ate of their flesh and drank of their blood. I sacrificed, in my first year, many who offered themselves to me, calling me Messiah and Visionary.

But it was the Necromancer, the one who taught me these things, who brought me together with the others of the Chymerical Circle, to whom I owed my absolute allegiance.

It was he, my brother's bones in his hands, hearing the words of my brother, that brought him to seek me out, to send the Chymerians to find me in Manchester and to engineer my arrival in London, into a new life, through the Pandemonium. To raise the specters of old, to speak with Lucifage and Abaroeth and the Angel Azriel, and to understand the Veil and its denizens.

Of all these things, it is the power it has granted me that will remain with me forever, until the day I cross over into the Veil's milky shore.

And there, I will find him, my Necromancer, my Lord, my Master.

But until then, I will do as I have been asked.

I will find the treasures of the earth. I will raise great wealth. I will perform the sacrifices necessary.

And I will build the portal of the Veil one day, and keep it open unto the Earth and let the devourers of that realm enter this world and keep dominion over it.

Visionary Four

After the final of the six sacrifices, I squeeze two drops in each eye, just beneath the eyelid, and I close them once, to let the Veil enter my bloodstream by way of my vision.

I open my eyes again. Their moist orbs burning with the acid of the Veil. I see the world turn to a foggy whiteness. Coming through its milky domain, a young man. He is roughly my age and resembles me so much it is like looking into a mirror.

I go to embrace my brother.

He whispers words that I can barely understand.

"What?" I ask.

He opens his mouth, which is filled with small worms and beetles crawling over his teeth, swarming up from his throat. They fly out from him, into the whiteness surrounding us, and they come toward me. I accept them, and through them I understand what he has wanted to let me know across the years between life and death.

The knowledge fills me with dread, for it was I myself who was destined to find the devil and his henchman. I was marked even as a child.

My father had not murdered my brother, nor had my mother.

"Carry me to the water, look, and know the truth," the voice had told me as a child when I'd first dug up my brother's grave.

When I had looked into the water, I had seen my own reflection. That was what I had been meant to see. To know the truth.

It was I, even as a baby, who had turned in our blanket, using some implement unknown to me, some small sharp tool left by my father nearby, that I had used to break open my twin's skull, and steal his life. To leak his brains onto my shoulder even as I held him, struggling, in our birth-cradle.

My first human sacrifice to the gods of the Veil. They were there then, somehow, watching me. Watchers. Guiding my hand.

The mystery that has dogged my steps is answered. The reason my father despised me and my mother prayed for my soul.

The mystery is no longer mystery. It is known to me. And understood.

I have seen the face of Baphomet, and it is the same face that I saw in the river when I was a boy. *Carry me to the water, look, and know the truth.*

I am Cain, himself. I am the very Beast.

THE NECROMANCER

I am the Monster. I am now the Necromancer himself.

A ystyrio, cofied.
Let him who reflects, remember.

Afterword

Beware the Afterword to a novella—if you must explain your intent, you're doomed. Yet, still, doomed though I may be, I must. *The Necromancer* is part of a cycle of stories and novels about Harrow and those who took part in its haunting. Harrow is a manse that sits upon a shadowed property of the Hudson Valley of New York. The novels of Harrow, so far, are *Nightmare House*, *Mischief*, *The Infinite*, and *The Abandoned*. *The Necromancer* is a tale of the creator of Harrow, Justin Gravesend, and is simply the beginning of his life as he moves toward the darkness that brings him to create the evil house with the potential for the greatest number of hauntings and occult phenomena.

Each of the Harrow tales is based simply on my idea of capturing the essence of a certain literary love of mine within the crucible of a magical place—in this case, Harrow. With *Nightmare*

House, it was the quiet ghost story that drew me to it; with *Mischief*, the coming-of-age tale; with *The Infinite*, the psychic investigation of a haunted place; and with *The Abandoned*, the all-out violence and mayhem and shocking moments, as if apocalypse has been unleashed.

With *The Necromancer*, the tale is of the debauched Victorian Englishman—or Welshman, in Justin's particular case—who embarks on a dark journey into madness and the deep end of the occult.

Each Harrow novel is as different from the one before as it is from the one after—I hope you'll enjoy exploring this gothic cathedral of a haunted world in the other Harrow novels.

—*Douglas Clegg, October 2005*

DOUGLAS CLEGG
THE ABANDONED

There is a dark and isolated mansion, boarded-up and avoided, on a hill just beyond the town of Watch Point in New York's Hudson Valley. It has been abandoned too long and fallen into disrepair. It is called Harrow and it does not like to be ignored. But a new caretaker has come to Harrow. He is fixing up the rooms and preparing the house for visitors....

What's been trapped inside the house has begun leaking like a poison into the village itself. A teenage girl sleeps too much, but when she awakens her nightmares will break loose. A little boy faces the ultimate fear when the house calls to him. A young woman must face the terror in her past to keep Harrow from destroying everything she loves. And somewhere within the house a demented child waits with teeth like knives.